To Moz for your support

The Clydesdales
are Getting
Restless

Dav

By

David D. W. Kingsmill

Cataloguing in Publication Data

Kingsmill, David D. W.

      The Clydesdales are Getting Restless

ISBN 978-0-557-16571-1

Content: 7813026

The first draft of this book was published in 2009 by m*agi*can*a* ISBN 978-0-9780675-7-1

David Kingsmill can be contacted at david@dkci.ca

For Cielo Bingley

whose wise pragmatism overruled my resignation

and introduced me to the medical team that would save my life.

and

for Gary Slaight,

my publisher and blind friend

ACKNOWLEDGMENTS

This book was initially published by Gary Slaight when it was in its first draft state. At the time I had inoperable liver cancer and didn't have the strength to do the necessary rewrites all books need. He thought it should be published before I croaked, at least for my friends. The result was a hardcover edition that I inflicted on everyone in my database, many of whom sent me lengthy edits and advice, most of which I found sound. I offer here my thanks to all for reading it, and profound apologies to anyone who was offended by the language or the deathbed imposition.

I would like to especially acknowledge Adrian Bayley who, when he'd read it, said "Well, I wouldn't recommend anyone buy it," and then told me why. He likes it now, he says. He could, of course, be lying.

CHAPTER ONE

The guy downstairs just killed someone, the bastard. You know how a cat wails in the middle of the night and it sounds like a crying baby, and no matter how many times you've heard it before, you can't get to sleep until it stops? Well, that's how it started, softly at first, then louder and clearer and, like always, I tried to sleep, but the cries became older, in a full wide-mouth, flapping-uvula sort of way. I won't lie to you, it was creepy. My eyes inflated. I throttled the pillow. It got worse. The screams broke up into shorter whooshes, like gasps, maybe cries muffled by ~~stinky~~ socks stuffed in a mouth, maybe gaging from blood shooting down a throat. You think a thousand things like that about sounds on the other side of a wall or from the basement. Then came a heavy thump that shook the floor, like a sack of water on wood, which is how I knew it was downstairs. And then silence. That was the creepiest. Silence isn't nothingness, you know. Silence is the sound of high-pitched hisses and ringing in dead air. Then they fade away and leave you all alone with the imagined gore.

I've never seen a wife or a kid or anyone else going down there with him so he could have killed a cat, a big one, but you know how these things are, it doesn't really matter. He killed something and in the scheme of things these days, people get just as crazy about cat killers as they do about kid killers. Either way it'll be all over the TV and they'll ask who turned the bastard in and they'll identify me. I'll be tied up in the legal process and media circus for God knows how long and I'd probably have to explain why I'm living alone in this expensive place, I'm only 18, I haven't got a job, and there are seven and a half new fishing rods, dozens of bars of stolen soap and shampoo from the Four Seasons' Hotel, a $3,000 freshly dry-cleaned clown's suit, and about $75,000-worth of gold wafers under my bed frame. And if they dig a little deeper and find out what I've been up to for the last few weeks, they're bound to wonder about all the dead guys.

It's all so deflating. If I call the cops, it'll change everything. It'll change me. But the whole point is to grab destiny by the balls and be the one who decides what's going to happen to me, if only for a few more weeks, not the other way around. Like, if I choose to take a boat down a river and it sinks, but I survive despite the fact I can't swim very well, the whole experience is bound to change me, right? At the very least, I'd think about it. Maybe even have nightmares. I might never go near a river or a boat again. I might take swimming lessons or learn to float on my back for hours. I might kill the dickhead captain who sunk the boat in the first place. The point is, did I change because I *chose* to go on the boat, or did I change because of what happened *after* I went on the bloody thing? I'd like to think I changed because I made the choice of going on the boat, as retarded a decision as that is given my propensity to sink. I have lead in my bones. An aunt once told me I looked very peaceful on the bottom of the lake just before she jumped in to save me and broke her ankle. That put a crimp in her tennis career. My sinking, it changed her, but it was her choice to jump in and save me so I shouldn't feel bad about it, should I? She did something of her own free will and it changed her. But I still feel bad about it, so this is not a black and white thing. It requires a bit of thought.

This destiny stuff isn't simple. I know these two guys in school, Chinky Chen and Injun Joe, nice guys but way too smart for most people to hang around with. Right from the start of school someone called them Chinky Chen and Injun Joe and it stuck. They didn't mind. They said so. I called them that, too, until one day when I was introducing them to a new kid at school and the principal was right behind me, but that's another story and I really haven't got time now, except to say the school secretary said I was the only student who ever noticed that the principal had redecorated his office five times in three years and could actually name the color changes. She was right. I sort of always see little things and remember them. Anyway, after that I look around first before I introduce them to anybody.

Anyway, these two guys play chess as if it's a regular board game that anyone can play. It's not. It's hard to play chess. I know how but I might as well just overdose than play with either of them. You are going to lose and who wants to play a game when you know the outcome every time? They also do something completely weird; they debate about philosophy. They never argue, they never fight, they *debate*. I figure this is the key to their social isolation; who wants to hang around in public with a debater?

Chinky Chen is the guy who says your worth in life is how you are perceived by others, not how you think of yourself. It's like talking into a tape recorder. The first time you hear your voice played back, you'd swear it was someone else. It doesn't sound a bit like you but, apparently, other people think it does.

Injun Joe – by the way, he is not a Native American or anything but from New Delhi – talks about whether things and people and situations we experience are real things or things we interpret as real. And then to complicate things, he says reality might depend upon entities that we don't actually experience but those entities make experience possible, like Fate or God. Can't prove them, can't disprove them, but maybe these are the things that create our reality.

These two go on for hours about this stuff and they never raise their voices. I admit, I got interested but never said a word. Just listened. I figured one of them would win one day and I'd be there to get the answer. That's what I want. Answers. And I guess I'm still looking for them, which is why this guy killing something downstairs pisses me off. I'm pretty sure I can't ignore him and the thought of being evicted because of some selfish psychopath is disturbing. I really like this place. I want to stay, at least as long as I can.

Don't get me wrong, I like my parents' place, too, but I knew I had to get out of there when my father came home one night with three opera tickets. Three. The opera. Like I know shit from opera.

"Hey, kiddo, look what I've got?" he said, and held up the tickets. He had an expression I'd never seen before: Guilt weeping through a weak smile. Shit, he had nothing to feel guilty about but it was there, just the same. Right behind his eyes. It was awful. I couldn't say a thing, either. I would have made him feel even worse. Bloody doctors! They started this. God, it made me mad.

There's nothing wrong with parents taking their son to the opera . . . Actually, I'm lying. There is. Maybe a daughter. Maybe. But even that's a stretch unless the daughter is into singing in tongues in the shower, but if she starts doing that out of the blue at 18, I'd call an exorcist, not take her to the opera.

Now, I've got to be careful here because feelings could be hurt, but my parents had never included me in anything like this. They did their own thing and I was sort of like a pet. They loved me and kept me clean and dry, and they made sure I'd still be alive and well when they got back from some event or trip or whatever. It didn't bother me. Babysitters were, like, damned near live-ins until one of them, Judy, gave me a constant hard on and she knew it. She would bend way over and let me look down her shirt, or she would let her underwear ride up until I couldn't breathe, or she'd stroke my back as we walked somewhere and tell me I was so cute . . . Suddenly I didn't have babysitters any more. But that was then and this is now, and here's the thing: It was my father holding the opera tickets, not my mother. She was opera. *He* was football. It was disturbing in so many ways.

First, right out of the blue, he's asking me to join them on one of their nights out. Very weird and instantly uncomfortable. Worse, if you dressed me up in a suit, I could fit right in at the opera; I had two suits actually, a grey and a blue pinstripe with a vest and they both looked terrific on me. But see, that's the problem. Some kids look like football players whether they are or not, others like pool hustlers, and some like race car mechanics. And none of these guys would look comfortable at the opera. They'd look dragged there and bored. But I looked like somebody who *would* go to the opera. How pathetic is that? No one was going to say, "hey, you look like someone who'd like to go to a World Wrestling Championship." Nope. At a stretch you could put some Bermuda shorts on me with an IZOD sweater wrapped around my skinny waist and you might – and I say this with caution – *might* take me to a tennis match once, and only once because at some point I'd fall down those steep steps and roll into the Royal Box and crush the Queen's hat. I'm desperately trying to avoid the "nerd" word here but, really, it fits.

All this is probably why Chinky Chen and Injun Joe let me listen in on their philosophical debates. It's a little-known law of physics: Nerds attract. And now my father was, in effect, declaring I was opera-ish? Whatever happened to blind parental love, the kind where your father outright lies and says you look football-ish even when look opera-ish or, at the most, tennis-ish. And how do I know? Because he bought the tickets for my benefit and because he hates the opera. But here he was, holding up tickets to something he didn't want to see but also demonstrating just how little he actually knew me, let alone my involvement with the family in situations dating back eighteen years.

I didn't hold it against him, though. The bloody doctors, who don't know shit when they see it, made him believe that whatever was wrong with me was something he could have prevented and the insidious phony guilt fogged his mind.

I'll bet eventually everyone realizes who they really are and, after a lifetime of refereeing the fight between the ugly naked truth and the fictional Hollywood life in which we hide, we wind up at peace not being

Spiderman or some other hopeless fantasy. This is where I was after *The Opera Moment*. I looked opera but I wasn't. I was a nerd but only on the outside; I was never the roll over and play dead type of guy anyway. Inside, I didn't know exactly who I was but the *Opera Moment* pushed me to understand I didn't have time to play the make-believe game because lying, even to yourself, takes up way too much time and energy.

Oh, I didn't think then I was going to die like the crazy doctor said, or what my parents believed – it's common knowledge they mix up hospital records all the time, right? – but after the doctors got into the heads of my parents, atmospheric changes around the house erected a wall of mortality in front of my face. It didn't have an end date on it. But there it was anyway and it raised a hell of a lot of questions, like, if you can see the wall, how far away is it? Do you just walk forward and then you hit the wall – Bam! – you're dead? Are you fine until you reach the wall, or are you slowly dying the closer you get? If you start dying slowly, can someone tell you the signs to know when you actually start the process, and what they are when you're halfway there? Questions like that. All of which brings up the whopper: Who do you ask to answer them? And more frustrating, if someone gives you an answer, can you believe it? Can he prove it? Exactly.

So after mulling all that around for a bit I deported the whole death and dying thing and went back to the point where I realized I would never be Spiderman. And once I'd done that, I felt entirely comfortable thanking my father for the idea but I thought I'd give the opera a pass this time. He didn't look hurt, maybe even a little relieved. He handed my mother all three tickets, rubbed my head and walked away.

But it wasn't just *The Opera Moment* that convinced me I had to get out of the house. It was also the constant, "How are you feeling?" question from my mother, asked in a squeaky voice with a defensive tilt of her head, the same pose and voice she used to ask the car dealership how much it was going to cost to repair the Jaguar after another crash. Until me, that was about the only uncomfortable moment she faced in her life. But to clarify, maybe I should tell you about *The Pho Moment* here.

About a week before *The Opera Moment*, my mother and I sat on the other side of this desk and this doctor, his name was Dr. Pho, looked down at a bunch of papers and said something about it being serious and I'd have a couple of months, maybe more, maybe less. And from then on I didn't pay much attention. My mother did, though. She leaned into Pho's desk and her eyes went round suddenly, like a big piece of food got stuck in her throat. That's when I started just looking around.

I recognized the painting behind Pho's head; it was a Monet and I'd seen it in some gallery somewhere, but this was a copy and a damned bad one, too. You could see it was only a little better than a poster in a frame and I figured the frame was worth way more than the picture. And then I looked around his office and saw that the wallpaper was stained near the window, which looked out onto a really depressing-looking parking lot with one spindly little tree that you could probably cut down with a steak knife if you worked hard on it, and beyond that an industrial park with these two-storey boxes lined up row after row with huge company signs nailed to the walls where cars drive by. All these buildings were exactly the same except for the signs which screamed, "I'm different! I'm not *Flakyboard Inc.*next door, I'm *Worldwide Extruded Plastic Inc.!*" Where do these companies get the bucks to have these signs made up, anyway? I'll bet they cost a fortune. And for what? I don't think anyone gives a shit and I doubt one in a hundred knows what a Flakyboard is.

And I thought: Who's this doctor trying to kid, anyway? Here he is in this tiny office overlooking a wasteland of an industrial park. Did he really believe that his patients would think he had the real deal with this Monet, and if he did, did he think it would make people believe he was right about his diagnoses? For Christ's sake. He was the fifth doctor we'd seen to tell us why I had a nose bleed. I knew why it wouldn't stop bleeding, I picked it one day with a very sharp fingernail and then it got into my sinuses and it wouldn't stop bleeding and my mother saw spots of blood on my pillow. Big, hairy deal. It'd stopped now, hadn't it? It had stopped weeks earlier.

Our family doctor had looked at my nose and said it looked okay but my mother insisted something horrible was wrong so the family doctor, a great guy actually, referred me to someone else, who referred me to some other doctor, who ran all these tests on me and then, when he wasn't *exactly* sure what he found, sent us to this Pho guy, "the" Go-to Guru for the University Hospital's Go-to Nose Bleed doctors, who was now saying something that horrified my mother. Come on! This was bullshit. But that's what started the, "How are you feeling today?" mantra from my mother who, until then, never knew where I was or what I was doing, and I don't think cared all that much as long as I didn't get into trouble, went to school every day and passed, didn't get some girl pregnant – that was a big thing with her; if only she knew – all because she had lunches and charities and spa treatments to go to and if I were a twisted kid, it would seriously disrupt her schedule.

Bloody doctors. They don't know shit, you know, but people still listen to them and rearrange their entire lives.

Anyway, I'd been thinking about making a break for it. Not just from my parents but everybody. As far as I knew, nobody had a clue what was going on except my parents and the dubious medical profession, and I didn't want anyone at school finding out because that would cause all sorts of problems. Exactly what problems I didn't know, but I figured it would seriously complicate my life. The only positive thing would be if girls lined up to give me one or two mercy fucks but even that thought didn't sit right because I was fine, felt fine, never better, actually, and I'd have to act pathetic to make it look real, and inevitably, they'd ask, "are you feeling okay?" and that would be *way* too creepy. But it did give me something to think about, especially a realistic shot at Denise Bleeker. Now there's a number! Gorgeous. Tits, ass, legs, the whole package. And she was nice, too. I mean, she'd never give it up for me under normal circumstances, but she was always nice to me, you know? She wasn't snobby. She actually talked to me. And if she thought I was going to die, she would probably be the first in line because that's the way she was. Nice. But I just couldn't do that to her. Inevitably, they'd find the right medical records and realize *The Pho Moment* was actually a crock, she'd think I'd made up the whole thing just to get into her pants, and I'd feel terrible about it.

Making a clean break would get me away from any *Moments* that might crop up, old or new. That was a good thing. I'd already come to understand that *Moments* are usually imposed on you, they come from out of nowhere and change your life without your permission. It's not like you're discovering something yourself, it's more like homework: "Read pages 236 to 275 tonight and tomorrow we'll talk about why the

Reformation changed your life." This is not discovery, this is being forced to learn shit no one believes they will ever need to know. Luckily my parents had to concede that since school was a non-issue now, discovery was the only intellectual pursuit left.

"Discovery" the big umbrella concept. Exactly what I would discover, even what I *wanted* to discover, was a bit of a problem. When the old explorers set out to discover something, they already had a goal, right? Columbus wanted to pillage The New World. Vikings obviously thought cod was a big deal. It's not. And go figure Marco Polo? He went all that way and brought back spaghetti. I'd have strung the guy up. But coming up with a discovery goal is very difficult. It's like asking a two-year-old, "what's it going to be, meds or law."

At this point I figured I was just fine, even though this Pho quack had my parents convinced otherwise. A number of times "denial" had been gently suggested as a normal phenomenon but dropped as soon as my eyes rolled. Now, however, I realized I could use this their belief that I only had a few months, maybe weeks, to let me go it alone for awhile. The argument would go like this:

What do you say when an old guy dies? Usually, "he led a good life," or, "he had a full life." The adult dead guy is always talked about in the past tense because it's assumed he's done it all or at least a lot of it. It may be sad for a lot of people but, really, it's natural for him to die. But what do you say when a kid dies? "It's a terrible tragedy." See? You talk about him in the present tense because a kid's death is unnatural and you don't want him to disappear, even if he's a stranger you only read about in the newspaper. Age is everything. He never had a chance to live and experience life. If an 18-year-old dies, he's on the edge of adulthood.

He won't get to experience "his potential" and the worst part is that he's at an age when he knows it. That's got to be torture. If the kid is given some warning, however, and he doesn't *have* to sit around and mope about it, shouldn't he be allowed to cram as much as he can into his life, experience whatever he can? How can that be wrong?

That's just about what I said except I used the word "innocent" to describe the dying kid, which made my mother wince, and "wicked" to describe all the things the old guy probably did in his life and, believing there is a better place beyond his personal hell, went. That resonated with my father, although he tried to hide it.

And it worked.

I won't bore you with all the negotiations. Suffice it to say my parents acted pretty much how you'd expect parents to act, thinking of a million possible perils and solutions including the bowel-twisting horrors of anyone who didn't eat vegetables. The trickiest one was the anonymity clause I insisted upon. My reasoning was that if I were to experience everything by myself, then I had to be alone and make choices as choices became necessary. I couldn't be tied to anyone, including my parents. I had to literally start my life all over again and not have someone looking over my shoulder. When I said this, I figured my parents would think of specific things, like me going to strip clubs or brothels, as if I knew where a brothel was, but what I emphasized were general things. I had to live an entire life in a very short time: be born, grow up, experience all kinds of normal stuff, and then, die, but I couldn't do that with someone hanging on, except for the last stretch. I'd be home for that, I assured them. In the end I had to concede meaningless gestures: a cell phone to be used only in emergencies by either party, doing nothing illegal, eating vegetables, that sort of thing. In return, I got the cashed-in university tuition annuity, and a private line of credit beyond that in my own bank just in case (like for bribes a landlord might need to rent to someone my age without references). I also got a promise of no e-mails ever. You cannot even pretend to be alone if you have e-mail. So there it was, then. Done. Now I had to get a place to live.

Finding a place is not something you are taught in high school but you should. You have to learn trigonometry for . . . what? To cross the street while figuring out the distance between two light poles? You learn all about how the Romans conquered Gaul for . . . what? To reinforce the fact that everyone has conquered France and the next conqueror could be . . . us? But if a school teaches you how to build a house so you have a roof over your head, or how to make a perfect egg salad sandwich, stuff you really need to know, it doesn't mean squat with an Ivy League university. Before you can get into Princeton or Harvard, you have to learn that no one really knows how the Pyramids were built, that Rosencrantz and Guildenstern are dead, and how ancient languages teach you how to spell, even though we have Spell Check. This hit me when I started to look at the classifieds and fliers to get an idea about house prices.

If they're not going to teach you how to spot a solidly built house without penalizing your future education, the least they could do is teach you what the hell the real estate market is all about. I mean, it's business, right? And the Harvard business school MBA is as big as Harvard Law. Shacks are going for half a million bucks, for Christ's sake, but if they don't tell you how one is built, you can't really tell if it's going to fall down right after you write the cheque. If they taught you real estate, however, you could assess the damned thing as a business investment. It sure would help. I never thought about how much my parents' house was worth but holy shit, it must be way more than $2 million compared to these one-bedroom, half-a-million-buck wooden jobs that look like some ignorant kid like me slapped together in a week and a half.

If they taught real estate, at least we'd know why all this math crap is a good idea to learn.

Buying a house was way out of bounds, so rental it would have to be. I didn't want to live in a really scuzzy area but nothing too good because my parents or their friends could live nearby and spot me one day. That would blow the anonymity thing. So I made a list, got a map and borrowed my mother's car and drove around and made some notes. I saw parts of the city I'd never seen before.

It's big, Toronto is. There's a whole shitload of parks but they're all different. They all have grass – or what passes as grass these days since weed killers are banned – and trees and benches, but the people in the parks really make the difference. One park downtown, Allan Gardens, has all these drunks sprawled around drinking out of paper bags. The crazy thing about that one is it also has this huge greenhouse filled with beautiful flowers and trees. It's run by the city, which is run by the geniuses who closed shelters for bums downtown and complain about them hanging around the park. Inside the greenhouse it's a riot of color. Outside the drunks are blah brown or grey. It kinda makes you blink. Another park, the one near the Art Gallery of Ontario, has guys around my age *and* bums with paper bags. Way out west, older guys throw stone balls around, sort of outdoor bowling, I guess. Way out east, they throw sandwich bags of 8-ball crack at each other and don't give a shit about the cops driving by and, it seemed, the cops don't give a shit about them. Weird as hell.

After all this driving around, I figured I should get a place where the people in the park were more like me. That way, I wouldn't stand out. I'd fit in. I'd be anonymous. And it was a perfect theory until the guy downstairs killed the kid, or the cat, or whatever, but that was way later.

CHAPTER TWO

Really, from the time I found the place until the bastard downstairs screwed things up, I had everything pretty well under control, although it wasn't without challenges. Furniture shopping for instance. It was harder to get the Mobilia Shoppe furniture guy to treat me like an adult than to re-stuff a fart.

What a name for a furniture store, eh? Half Italian, half French, they soak you in both languages. If some lady walks in there wearing more than two carats on her finger, the salesmen clamp onto her like lamprey eels on a fish. God forbid someone like me would have the nerve to shop there. Young, stupid, no money, no taste, and male. I couldn't help the male part but I could work on the rest.

The first thing a salesman looks at are what kind of shoes you're wearing and if they're clean. On someone my age, they've been trained to look for penny loafers. Not sneakers. Not even skateboard shoes. Penny loafers. They put you in the right category: monied. Forget about the fact that Weejuns are *so old,* these guys don't know that. You can't tell them, either, because it contradicts what they learned from older salesmen who learned from even older guys, and they never learn anything new because the neurons going through their brains are about as fast as wrinkled seniors in a swimming pool of peanut butter. My Weejuns cost half as much as my skateboard shoes. See? They just don't get it. So I polished up the Weejens before I went. And no socks; that really says money to these jerks. Once they've scoped out the shoes, they look for the IZOD label or the Land's End or LL Bean button-down Oxford-cloth shirt and I went for the off-white IZOD under the brass-button blue blazer with the jeans. I felt like a complete traitor to anyone I've ever liked but, really, I haven't got a lot of time to screw around with these things so I swallowed my cred and went.

I knew, *I just knew* I was going to run into an asshole in that store and sure enough, the guy who approached me had this smarmy grin on his face like I was some kid completely lost in the Stock Exchange or a strip club, except I've been to a strip club and I wasn't the least bit confused. But he had this voice, this 'tude, like he was going to pat my head and give me a gold star if behaved like the good child he hoped I was.

"May I help you, Sir?"

Now come on, no one is going to call an 18-year-old "Sir" unless he's jerking you around. If I'd gone to one of those discount places where you buy a sofa that in two months of minimal use the legs fall off and the springs pop right through the polyester cushions, a salesman would be all over me with cheesy lines like, "it's perfect for you, man! This is exactly what you're looking for, I can tell, and I know my sofas,

Bud, and this is a deal, a real steal, but only today. Price goes up tomorrow so you'd better make up your mind fast. We've only got this one left."

But at The Mobilia Shoppe, it's like you have to prove to the guy you're worthy by knowing what you're looking at. And not just me. I was there with my mother once and saw someone with less than two carats get the same treatment as me. So take my word for it, a, "may I help you" line is bullshit. He wants *you* to help *him* make a living, and a good one, too, without a lot of trouble or rush, Heaven forbid.

"I'd like to see Sectionals,"

"Sectionals?" he said, as if he knew he hadn't cleaned out the sand before making creamed spinach and was waiting for you to take a bite.

"You have Sectionals, right?" I wasn't self-conscious about this. When you're only 18, you might say something like "Sectionals" and think, 'whoa, maybe I've got that all wrong, maybe they're called something else,' because whenever you do something for the first time that older people do, you get doubts, but I knew what they were called because my mother and I were in there once, that's what she wanted for the basement, and she said, "Sectionals." She's three carats, by the way. Two guys showed her these sofas that went together in a half square and it was the reason I was there now because I knew they had them. I could have asked my mother if I could borrow the one in the basement but I didn't want to go there. I wanted my own. I thought it would be less hassle. This salesman, though, was making me think again.

"Sectionals, Sectionals, let me see, yes, I believe we have a few," he said. And then he just stood there and looked at me with that smarmy grin, as if it were a chess game and it was my move.

I remembered something my father said to a banker who kept making bad loans to restaurants: "It's okay," I said, "you can't be an expert on *everything*. Sectionals must be a specialty, like brain surgery. You wouldn't ask a barber to do brain surgery. And no reputable barber would attempt it, so maybe you could introduce me to someone who knows all about Sectionals?"

He didn't expect a challenge from a kid. I could see his brain banging off the inside of his skull. His hands formed a prayer Tee Pee in front of his chest, lines on his forehead disappeared, his upper torso bent forward at the waist and his head tilted slightly to the left. If he'd been older, he would have farted, or worse, but he was maybe 40 and instead losing sphincter control, his lips just flapped two or three times as he cleared his throat like a horking camel. I was in Egypt once. I've heard a camel cough. It's hilarious.

"Oh, I'm sure I can help you now that I think about it more clearly. I'm afraid I'm a little foggy this morning. I think I'm coming down with something," he said.

I took a quick step back and gave him a look like I'd seen brain matter dribbling out his ears. "Jeezes, man, I didn't come here to contract *boogaphalia!*"

"No, No, I'm fine, really. Just a tickle in my throat."

"Are you sure you haven't got *boogaphalia*? It's going around, you know. Don't you watch the news?"

"Yes, yes, of course I do. I don't have any of the symptoms."

"You sure?"

"Absolutely."

"How do you know?"

"I, ah, wrote them down when I saw the story on TV."

"So no rectal itch or any anal leakage?"

"No!"

"Bleeding gums, spinning eyes, dizzy spells, yellow toe nails?"

"Really, sir, I'm just fine. Really. I wash my hands all the time, ten or twelve times a day. See?" he said, and put his hands out, palms up, like my mother flashing her nails.

I didn't say a thing. I just looked him up and down like I was checking out the way he was dressed. And I was. For instance, he had one of those fake gold Rolex watches that cost fifteen dollars from a suitcase salesmen at Yonge and Bloor. You can always tell because the second hand of a real Rolex sweeps smoothly around the dial. His didn't. His shoes were those clunky squaretoed things that could have been plastic as well as leather, with soles that surround the uppers like tug boat bumpers. I don't want to sound like a snob but I hate those things. They look good strapped to a pair of skis but nowhere else. Ah, Jeezes, I *do* sound like a snob saying that, but really . . . Otherwise he was neutral. He wouldn't clash with anyone walking into that store. He was invisible, bland and, at this moment, was betraying the fact that he was emotionally conflicted. He quietly groveled in slow motion like a commissioned salesman in a funeral parlor while twitching to be somewhere else.

He couldn't help looking at his fake watch. I'd gotten there at about 11 o'clock and by the time I'd jumped up and down on four or five of these expensive Sectionals and had this guy turn them upside down so I could check out his boast about "solid hardwood, handcrafted frames, made with wooden dowels, not screws," it was about noon and I guess it was time for his lunch. I could see that in a place like that, where they don't have to have too many customers to make a living because everything costs so stinking much, you could get into the habit of eating at exactly the same time every day. If you do that, your body starts to expect it. If something upsets the rhythm, you might get stomach cramps. Now that I think about it, he was probably terrified it was the first sign of *boogaphalia*. Me? I'd had a bagel with smoked salmon and garlic herb cream cheese with red onions and alfalfa sprouts just before heading up to the store so, I was good, but this guy was getting rude.

"I kinda like this one" I said, patting the cushions of the one he'd just turned upright. "What do you think?"

"Oh, yes," he said, "that's the one I'd choose."

"Okay, let's think about it then. It's got to go with a coffee table, some side tables, lamps and a farting chair."

"A what?" His head tilted and his upper torso lurched forward again. I thought I saw a little bead of sweat on his forehead but I had to look away to stop laughing. I was glad I didn't have a mouthful of water.

"A farting chair. You don't have one?" I had to look away again. Shit, I was having fun.

"Ah, I'm not sure . . ."

"You're married then?"

"No, no, I'm not," he said.

"You got the time?"

He looked at the lead-paint Rolex. "Twelve fifteen."

"You got to be somewhere?"

"No, no, why?"

"You keep looking at your watch."

"No, no, I'm all yours. Nowhere to go."

"Any kids?"

"No, no, I'm not married. I said . . . didn't I?"

"It's got to be well stuffed and cocoon-like so you never want to get up."

"What?"

"A farting chair. But it can't be leather. It has to be a fabric that breathes easily. You don't want your bare ass sticking to it in summer. It also should be browny-grey, especially on the arms where you grab on and squeeze when you're straining, because that'll hide the dirt from your hands. Otherwise, you wouldn't need it in the first place."

"A farting chair?"

"That's what I said, isn't it?"

"I've never heard of such a thing. I'm certain we don't have one *here.*"

"I'm sure you do. You probably call it something else. It's a big chair with a high back, big arms. You see them in movies, old movies, especially British ones when the old geezers sit in clubs and smoke cigars and drink brandy. Except those are always leather and, like I said, you don't want leather because you'll want your friends to sit there naked if they want and you don't want their skin to stick. And a fart in one of those will just bubble up and make a slapping noise. You want fabric so the fart is muffled and filtered through the bottom. That way it won't smell, either. But, really, if it's fabric, you've got to put that stuff on it so it'll wipe down. Scotchguard, I think they call it. Sometimes they look a little plain but a farting chair can't be, like, modern or anything because this is for sitting in, not looking at. Some dorks call them easy chairs."

"Ah, an easy chair. Yes, yes."

Bing . . . fucking . . . go.

So he showed me some easy chairs and I had him turn them upside down so I could see the wooden dowels, which I couldn't because I didn't really know what dowels were, and then I got him to show me some tables. I liked the glass coffee table with the chrome around it but, really, I'd have to buy Windex to keep it clean and probably couldn't put my feet up on it while I watched TV. So I went for a light oak, which went with the Sectional. And I got matching side tables and a couple of lamps. By this time his eyes were opening and closing like a ventriloquist's dummy. I think I heard his stomach bubble.

"And I'll need a bed," I said.

"A bed?"

"Yeah, like the one I saw in the window, that sleigh bed."

"Oh, that's a beautiful bed!" he said. I knew that. The price tag was insane.

"But I don't want the mattress or the box spring, just the wood sleigh frame thing."

"Actually it comes as one unit. The mattress set is the finest you can buy."

"You don't say. How much would that be worth on its own?"

"I would hazzard to suggest the mattress and box spring are somewhere around the three thousand dollar mark. But the entire bed is only selling for about five."

"Okay, well, take the three grand off, keep the mattress thingies and you've got a deal."

"Oh, I don't think I can do that," he said. His face was a riot. It was if someone had injected Botox into his lips to create a permanent grimace and a plastic surgeon had pulled the rest of his face behind his ears.

"Okay, well, forget the whole thing, then," I said, and started for the door.

"Wait! Please wait! Let me talk to the manager!"

"Okay, but could you make it fast? I'm hungry." The guy reverted into the lip- flapping state.

I was going to ask whether I could get a discount for cash and then give him a credit card once he'd made up the bill but I couldn't bring myself to be that much of a prick. He said he could have it delivered in two days, which was fine, because then I went to this rug store, Boteh, and bought a huge silk oriental, and finally to that chain store where I bought one of those number beds, the one Rush Limbaugh and some Babe worth six million dollars are always going on about, and both stores said they could deliver in two days, as well. And then I went to the electronic store and bought one of those humongous flat screen plasma babies with surround-sound, but only if they delivered and set it up the next day, which they did because the guy there worked on commission and I said I'd cancel if it didn't turn up. It did.

Anyway, it all worked out as planned and it was fabulous. I fell asleep on the Sectional watching football and drooled all over the pillow so then it was truly mine, and I won't lie to you, that carpet on the wooden floor is so silky and warm on your bare feet you get a real appreciation for those Persians. No matter what politicians say, Persians rule! The bed's fabulous, too. And huge. King size. I was lying there propped up on the pillows looking down at the foot of the bed and figured you'd have to have at least two Clydesdales side by side to pull a sleigh that big. Awesome. I've got it all configured, too. I'm Sleep Number 52 on one side and 74 on the other, depending upon where I ache. It's that good. But I guess there's a price to pay when you don't buy everything matching, like the mattress and the frame, because it seemed like it was a bit warped. It didn't lie absolutely flat on the frame. It made a tiny thump sounds when you jumped on it.

Even though I think I got the better of the Mobilia Shoppe guy, it still didn't seem satisfactory somehow. I mean, I bought a shit load of stuff but, after I'd paid, he somehow made it seem like he was doing me a favor, as if he were just amusing me until someone more adult came along. Why wouldn't he treat me just like anyone else? What makes someone adult? Grown up? Is money the mark? As soon as I paid, I was right back to being a kid. But before then I controlled him. What's up with that? When you're on your own, is it necessary, or better, to be an adult? I thought maybe yes. Maybe. I'd have to think about it some more.

Anyway, after that everything went pretty well and stayed that way until that bastard downstairs killed the kid, or the cat, or something.

CHAPTER THREE

You've got to have a couple of stable things in your life so you're not always watching over your shoulder: a roof over your head, a bed to sleep in, and food. I had the main floor of a house on Dovercourt just above College Street. Good place. A very comfortable bed. And the western edge of *Little Italy* was a block south and east with all the Italian restaurants, coffee bars with massive silver espresso makers, and outdoor patios to keep me fed and watered. Bonus. But as I sat up on my sleigh bed admiring the strength of the Clydesdales tethered to the footboard, pounding their hooves, snorting steam into the freezing air, something was missing:

I couldn't think of a goddamned thing I wanted to do, or *needed* to do.

When you've got no pressure you can think of all sorts of things. Ever since I was a kid I wanted to drive a race car. Well, that's great, but you've got to go to a track and actually learn how to drive F-1. No one is going to lend you a million dollar racing car to rip around a track if you have never driven one. Just like I always wanted to fly. Same thing. No time. You could always go out and rent a horse and ride it but who the hell wants to ride a horse? I was never into westerns. Go to India and see the Taj Mahal? My passport had expired and it would take forever to get a new one and besides I didn't have forever, apparently. Go on a road trip? Nah. What if you get stuck in some place like Galatin, Missouri, where the only worthwhile thing in whole town is a courthouse where they let one of the James Brothers off for robbery and murder but imprisoned another guy who founded a religion. Local priorities are fickle things you can't predict on road trips and they can spell trouble for white kids who look like they could go to the opera. Climbing Mount Everest? Well, first you need that passport, then probably some training. But most of all, you have to *climb up a mountain*. Mountains are high. High means cold. Cold is the shits. And getting so tired your legs give out and you can't breathe, why does anyone in their right mind want to climb a mountain? You've got to be a bloody nutbar.

The only thing that cheered me up was the possibility that whatever I came up with would be right out of the blue, like a surprise birthday party.

I was thinking about all this as I sat on my sleigh bed running through a series of porn I'd downloaded from my laptop. Great name for something to look at porn with: Laptop. Perfect except you can't smell the baby powder perfume on a computer stripper. All girls smell. Regular girls' bras heat up, the skin between their tits heats up and gets slippery, even their faces heat up. And each has her own smell, her own scent. I was thinking about this, fondly, as the Clydesdales stomped the ground.

So now I am surrounded by porn and still thinking about what the hell I *really* want to do that I couldn't do before, other than jerk off in privacy, which is actually very liberating. It took me all of about two days to realize I could scream obscenities without having to worry about giving my parents heart attacks.

One thing no one ever discusses is how much you can learn from porn sites, things like elasticity and weird tribal practices. Porn gives you useful ideas beyond the obvious. Mass marketing, for instance, or the significance of good lighting in photography, which is most apparent in the amateur sites, where they don't know shit from lighting but it gives the pics a sort of real life character. I fell in love with this blond on the alt.sex.binaries.co-ed site. She was thin, had breasts that weren't too big or too small, seemed actually thrilled to be taking it in one of her three primo body cavities. She had something like a complete package. She was a riveting presence. Of all the series and sites, I kept coming back to her. I couldn't take my eyes off her, or keep my hands to myself and at one point I swear I almost rubbed myself raw. I wanted more pictures, maybe her with another really cute girl but there were only 72 images in the series so I read the intro to see who she was, which I never do because it's all this type, which is not what you go to alt.sex.binaries newsgroups for. Her name was Petra. I damned near screamed.

For two years, I had a fake ID. Everybody did. If you didn't, you were a loser. I'd got it from a friend, who said he got it from a forger somewhere, and it had a really grainy picture of me on a driver's license and the same picture on a Health Card with a date that swore I was 19-years-old, the drinking age. It was good. Until now. It said my name was Petra Prince. Petra. If I had known was a girl's name, I would have broken into a cold sweat every time I walked into one of the three bars we used to hang around. We went to these places because they were well known at school for turning a semi-blind eye to underage drinking if you had fake ID, but it would have freaked me out if I'd known Petra was a girl's name. And now, looking at this stark-naked angel on the computer, I instantly felt betrayed, betrayed by my friend, betrayed by the forger, betrayed by the Internet universe. It's sickening when people all around the world are laughing at you. You know they are, but you can't hear them.

A flashy ad for Vegas vacations popped up on the screen to the upper right of legs-spread Petra, who I now realized was looking right at me and laughing. Vegas was out of the question – too far – but doing the James Bond thing in Niagara Falls was possible with ID.

Shit!

Technically I had one, of course, but now it was embarrassingly, nakedly untrustworthy. Why I deluded myself to believe my ID was bulletproof made me ponder my sanity, but what the hell was the world coming to when you go to all the trouble to do things you're not suppose to do and some perverse, sadistic bastard takes advantage of your ignorance of Easter European culture and gives you the name of a porn star? Honestly, there ought to be a law. To regain my dignity, I had to get a new ID.

I didn't know how.

When you grow up like I did, you just don't get into this kind of thing. People sort of hand things to you. I mean, the first time someone said they needed fake ID, my friend, sitting right beside me, chirped up that he could get him some. He had never told me he could do something like this. He was a good friend, for Christ's sake. You'd think a friend would confide in you that he was tied to the criminal elements of society. I mean, imagine the conversations you could have with someone tied to another world like that. Until then we just talked about what a bunch of ratshit bastards surrounded us: teachers, douche bags, Goths, crack heads . . . how were we going to get our hands on the latest video game . . . which girls would put out . . . what a bunch of losers the Maple Leafs were. That kind of thing. But knowing forgers? Now, that's off the charts.

So you see, my Petra ID just sort of fell in my lap in the first place. I didn't go out and look for it, I got it because I was simply there when the subject came up. All I did was say, "get me some, too, okay?" Fifty bucks and a week later I had it. Now that I thought about it again, fifty bucks was a lot of money. I wonder if he took a cut, maybe a large cut. Would he do that to his best friend? I slapped my forehead hard: *Duh!* He deals with the criminal element. Of course he would. I made a mental note to kneecap him if I ever saw him again.

Okay, I was bothered by this setback but not really pissed off. Like I said, things have always just popped into my lap when I've needed them, like magic, and I didn't see why it wouldn't happen again. Not just material things but answers to tricky problems like this ID thing. If I don't have an answer to something right away, I just put it aside and forget about it and go on to do something else. But I probably don't actually forget about it. It's there somewhere in the back of my alleged mind, mulling around on its own. I call it the *Mull Mode*. And later, when you're deep into doing something else, out pops the answer to whatever the problem was. That's the *Holly Cow Moment*.

Three of my teachers label my *Mull Moments* on report cards as "does not apply himself." The same three believe my *Holly Cow Moments* are cheating. No imagination.

Anyway, I didn't have an answer to the ID problem, and I figured I had gotten away with it for a long time so far, I'd just go into *Mull Mode* with that and go onto something else. Which happened to be food because I was hungry and there wasn't much in my place.

I've always been curious about where stuff you eat comes from. I think it started when I was in grade school and the teacher took us on a street car to a dairy, right in the middle of the city, where they bottled milk and made ice cream. I remember the smell of cold water on wet bricks and steel and the constant breeze from fans overhead and some guy in a doctor's coat opening a spigot and each of us getting a glass of milk. And then the same guy took us to the back where another guy in a white coat scooped vanilla ice cream into small paper cups and gave us little plastic spoons to eat it with. I remember how flimsy the paper cup was. And how cold the ice cream was.

On another class trip, we went to the Royal Agricultural Winter Fair – it's the largest in the world, you know – and we got to watch the cows and horses shit in their stalls, ducks and geese shit and squawk in their cages, and sample some fresh apple cider that some hefty lady in a truly ugly dress was making right there. God, that cider was good! You could buy a jug of it and I loved it so much I bought a gallon. A whole gallon. I could barely lift it up. I drank it all on the bus on the way back to school and puked in the parking lot. Never bought another glass of it again but funnily enough I still have fond memories of that day and the cider. If I had a kid, I think I'd buy him a gallon of apple cider from the Winter Fair but I'd dole it so as not to ruin his life later.

Despite the fact I suppose I've been privileged and my parents taught me why a steak at a good steak house is worth $45 and up, I've always liked more simple things. Spaghetti, for instance. I love spaghetti with meat sauce. Cheap. Simple. And with garlic bread, one of the best meals ever. The smell of garlic bread could lead me around a corner and into the arms of a pack of armed crack dealers. I won't lie to you, I couldn't prevent it. And roast chicken. A roast chicken, no stuffing, just baked until the skin is crispy and the potato chunks around it have soaked up the fat and are brown and crunchy on the outside and like porridge inside and the steam from the oven is thick with bubbling browning juice . . . . To me, that's heaven. I saw a cooking program that showed you how to make fresh spaghetti, so I know it's flour, water, a little oil, salt and maybe an egg, and then way too much time kneading it and rolling it out. And I don't particularly find it interesting how to feed beef parts into a grinder to make hamburger. But a chicken is another thing. How can a feathery bird with useless wings and the smell of wet cat crap and straw, be transformed into a bronzed, crispy-skinned gastronomic Stanley Cup with an aroma that makes you drool? I had to know. My mother once took me to downtown where she got her furs cleaned and stored, and on the way back she said we might as well take a detour and get a chicken from one of the butchers in an area called Kennsington. The place was on St. Andrews St. off Spadina and all it had was poultry. She said it was Kosher, "Jewish." Who knew a chicken could have religion? Anyway, it was the best chicken she ever roasted and she always promised that she would get another one when she went down to do the fur thing but I don't think she ever did because nothing again was quite like that Jewish chicken. Either that, or it was one of those memory tricks, the ones where you have something to eat and it's amazing but no matter how many times you try to have it again, it's never the same. Like Turtles, those chocolate and caramel-and-nut candies. At first they were fantastic, then years later, nothing really special. Or mandarin oranges at Christmas. One year they're a revelation and the next year you dive to the bottom of your stocking and rip them apart and they're mealy and tasteless. That's pretty alarming for a little kid, you know. You think something's gone wrong with you, not the orange. I'm afraid to have another sip of cider for that very reason; it would probably taste completely different from that first gallon.

I could go on but never mind, it was a chicken I was after, so I looked it up on the map and saw it was actually within walking distance. Sure enough, there it was, and it hadn't changed a bit, and just like the last time, it was practically empty. Jeezes, what a great city.

"So, I know this sounds stupid and all but what's the best way of cooking this?" I asked the guy behind the counter as he was plopping the thing in a white plastic bag. He looked at me like I was a bacon sandwich. He just tilted his head. No smile. Nothing.

"You roast it," he said.

"And?"

"Roast. Put it in the oven. Three fifty. Ninety minutes, until the legs wobble easily."

"Oh, right. Thanks," I said, and then, screwing up the courage I'd acquired since Dr. Pho started mumbling in his chintzy office, "look, as you can probably tell, I'm not exactly a food expert or anything but my mother bought one of these things a few years ago and it was amazing and I was wondering . . . why?"

Now the guy was grinning: "You're not Jewish, are you?"

"No, Anglican. I don't think we have chickens."

Now he laughed out loud. "Hey, Saul," he yelled down the length of the store. "You got any Anglican chickens down there for this guy?"

A guy wiping his hands on a bloody white apron, came walking toward the front. "What are you talking about?"

I didn't know whether to laugh along with this guy or get mad because he was making fun of me. "I just want to know what makes your chickens so good," I said to Saul.

"Seriously?"

"Seriously."

"You're not Jewish, then."

"No, I'm Anglican. Well, not a really big Anglican. I don't go to church or anything but I had to go through all that stuff with the Bishop when I was younger . . ."

"With the Bishop, eh? You should go to church again, young man," Saul said. "One day you will. We all do, one day."

"Chicken," I said. "What's with your chicken? Please."

Saul then explained the chicken bath to loosen the feathers (cool water so the outer layer of skin doesn't cook off first), the salting, the cooling in the refrigerator rather than in ice water, which stops diluting the taste. He took me to the back and showed me the salting bit but he wouldn't show me the feather machine, or the gutting, or the cooling. He introduced me to the salter, who was a rabbi. I knew Saul was kidding when he asked me when the bishop blessed the bacon, and asked me whether "it was good as sex." They all laughed at that and I did, too.

When I got outside with my chicken, I felt terrific. I had learned something, something practical, and somehow this whole education of being by myself seemed to be actually happening, even when mulling. Who knew? Not me. Not until then.

The sky was brilliant, cloudless, although the air was colder than the stare of a Canadian Security Intelligence Service agent after you start talking in school about atomic bombs, but I decided to walk around, since I was already there. The place was a warren of little streets with cars on the sidewalks delivering everything from slimy fish to fruit and vegetables. A cheese truck delivery guy, someone hauling sacks of nuts, and a Goth punker wheeling racks of clothes into a store, were all jabbering and yelling at people to get the hell out of the way. Around one corner a thick wall of plastic surrounded a patio of a tiny restaurant and a waft of garlic made my mind swell up in my skull. On the patio, huddled under coats, were three guys, a little older than I, with scruffy beards and smudged coats leaning into each other over cups. They didn't look like a den of thieves but it wouldn't have mattered anyway because I looked past the patio inside and at a table there were two girls, about my age, eating soup or something. They both sat with their legs crossed, thighs out, skirts all the way up to their asses, nice legs, cold legs, legs that should be kept warm, legs that . . . It was just after twelve noon. I walked in and sat at the long bar where I could see the patio outside, around the restaurant and down at the girls.

"You here to have lunch?" The voice belonged to the woman behind the bar whose mascara looked like asphalt road patches. I looked at her. Couldn't say a thing so I nodded? "I'll get you a menu," she said, and in seconds placed one in front of me. "Can I get you something from the bar, maybe a beer or something while you choose?"

Now *here* was something different, someone asking *me* if I wanted a drink without asking for *ID* rather than *me* asking for one, *before* dark, in a *restaurant*. I tried to be cool about this. "Yeah, sure," I said, pointing to one of the draft taps, "I'll have a Stella." She was smiling, just a little, but smiling, and looking at me straight on. Anyone who'd ever served me before looked with her head turned.

The place was French, that much I could tell. What everything was on the menu I couldn't tell you, but one word I recognized was the "soupe," so I ordered that. By the time it arrived, I'd finished the Stella and the bar lady asked me if I wanted another. Yup.

The soup was amazing. It was fish and I would *never* have ordered fish soup. Anywhere. For any reason. Until then, the thought of fish soup would have made me gag. But this soup was fantastic. It came with a cracker in the middle that was piled with green garlic guck and the soup was not at all fishy and I finished every single drop. By then it was about a quarter to one, I'd finished the soup and both Stellas and I was feeling absolutely great. God, this was the life. I sat there looking outside and only then realized the girls had gone and so, too, had the scruffy guys on the patio.

I felt warm all over. I was pissed, no doubt about it. When I breathed in, it seemed so easy. My ankles were warm underneath my socks; I remember that, it was so weird. The bar felt like a blanket around my shoulders. At one point I thought I would cry a bit.

"You okay, or do you want another?" the bar lady asked.

"Oh, what the hell," I said, "let's make it one more."

She looked at me with that little smile again but this time her head was turned a bit. "Say, you're of age, right?"

"Yeah, yeah, sure," I said. The way I said it, or maybe it was my face, I don't know, but her eyebrows went up.

"I know it's a bit late but could I see some ID?"

Shit. Oh, shit. "Yeah, sure, of course," I said, and pulled out my wallet.

"Get out of town!" she said, examining my driver's license. "Petra? Petra! That's a Russian girl's name." She looked at me through those thick black-rimmed eyes. "You could get my liquor license pulled." She looked around. "Luckily for you no one's in here but, are you nuts? How long have you been trolling on this one? How old are you really?"

To say I felt a little silly would be an understatement. "Eighteen. I've had that for quite a while."

"No shit," she said, and started to laugh. "I suppose you got another picture one, right?"

"Yeah," I said, and passed over the Health Card. I shouldn't have done that. She took both, picked up a pair of scissors and cut them up.

"Hey!" I said, trying to grab them before she could destroy my life. Too late. "Now what the hell am I going to do?"

"How long before you're of age, kid?" She asked.

"Awhile."

"Well, Petra, you're going to have to get some new ID, aren't you?"

I didn't know where this was going.

"Like the *soupe au pistou?*" she asked.

"Yeah. . . ."

"How was the service?" Her head was still cocked to one side.

"Ah, well, great."

"How great? I mean, how great in terms of a tip, Petra?"

"Twenty percent?" I said. She shook her head. "Thirty per cent?" Her mouth turned down.

"Try thinking in terms of actual dollars, Petra," she said, picking up a note pad and a pencil. She wrote down "50"and showed me.

"Fifty," I said, "fifty dollars?"

"Yeah, that seems fair,"and she wrote down an address on Church Street and a name, Ivan, underneath the "50." Then she gave me the bill, $22.90. I gave her $80 cash. "Change?" she asked.

I knew the answer. "No, that's okay. Who's Ivan?" I asked, pocketing the note.

"The best. Regular business hours. Turn around time is two days," she said, and then, "Bye, Petra, come back when you've seen Ivan, okay? Have a nice day." She took the empty Stella glass from the bar, gave me a wave, and then a 'shoo' motion with her hand. But she did it in a nice way. I knew I could come back.

Outside I didn't know whether to laugh or cry, be happy or mad. I had just had another *Holy Cow Moment* and they never fail to astonish and confuse me. I didn't know if I should go right over to the address on Church Street, and if it wasn't there, come back and confront the bar lady, or go home. I had the chicken, what I'd come down here for anyway, so I went home. But I didn't feel at all like seeing Petra there. In fact, on the way back, I decided to part company with her. She'd be erased. She'd go into the recycling bin. Even though she's probably still on alt.sex.binaries.co-ed, I decided never to go there again. I might go to other newsgroups but not *co-ed* again. It would be too embarrassing.

CHAPTER FOUR

Who knew something as simple as a chicken was going to change your life? I mean, if you could cook something *that* good at home, and *that* simple, you could probably live with a smile on your face forever. And who wouldn't like that? It got me thinking about all sorts of things I really like to eat, like egg salad sandwiches. The first time I had an egg salad sandwich it was like the heavens had opened up and I saw God. I loved it. And to top it off, I wasn't alone. A couple of days later – I swear, just a couple of days – I saw an old Woody Allen movie where these Japanese guys ran around trying to find the perfect egg salad sandwich. Okay, it was a comedy but this Allen guy obviously appreciated egg salad sandwiches as much as I did, maybe more, because he did a whole movie about them.

Has this ever happened to you? You're talking about something as bizarre as an egg salad sandwich and you hear everyone around you talking about egg sandwiches, or eggs, or movies with eggs in them. It happens to me all the time. I'll think of something completely weird like pet fleas and in the next two days pet fleas are all over the news. Before I left home, I watched an old movie on cable called *The Maltese Falcon*. Now, this movie was made way back, light years before I was born, and I'd never seen it before. But the next night, the very next night, some guy is on television saying *The Maltese Falcon* theme underscores the reason the monetary system around the world collapsed, because all the greedy characters in the movie except Humphrey Bogart were ruthlessly reaching for "the stuff of dreams." It freaked me out. I *never* understand *anyone* who talks about the economy. Never. But as soon as this guy started talking, I listened to it all – and remembered. How about that? Egg salad sandwich, Woody Allen. Maltese Falcon, world collapse. If this sort of thing doesn't happen to you, then the world must revolve around me, right? Only kidding.

My mother made me that first egg salad sandwich. As I think I've told you, she's three carats, which should also tell you she doesn't cook a lot. Sure, she can cook a chicken, and she obviously knows the right chickens to buy, and she does a good enough prime rib, but she makes pork taste like cardboard and, I suppose this is the mark, she's never cooked anything the same way twice. It's a consistency thing. She hasn't got it unless she has a recipe right in front of her and follows it until the sweat beads off her forehead, which she hates more than anything in the world. Sweating, that is. When she's at the tennis club, I think she stops playing when she starts to sweat, not when the match is actually finished. I don't think she or her friends care about the score, they stop when the sun's too hot or the martinis look cold. Anyway, she made that first egg salad and I begged her to make me another one the next day and she sighed and did but it wasn't the same. I don't think it was one of those memory things, either. It was the next day, for God's sake. It didn't taste the same. She said she had no idea why it was different, if it *was* different, and the way she said it indicated she thought I was an alien or something. I gave her one last try and damned if it didn't taste different from the *other* two. So I took a page from Woody Allen and ordered an egg salad sandwich in every restaurant I could for the next year or so, trying to find the perfect one. And I sort of did. In this deli in the Village, and it was the same every day, too. It wasn't perfect, but it seemed like it was going to be as close as I was ever going to get. Then the place closed and in its place this snap-and-crackle-clean organic vegetable market opened and you couldn't buy an egg salad sandwich. It was one of those days that make you think someone stole your wallet on the streetcar. You don't see it coming. You don't know where it happened. You don't know who did it. All you can do is grab your back pocket every second or two, hoping *you've* made a big mistake and it's still there. But it isn't. And it's more than a wallet, it's part of *you* that has been ripped from your body! It's the phantom egg salad sandwich recipe, something that might go down in history. It's gone.

This was, like, years before, but the egg salad sandwich thing lead to another revelation, one that seized me now: Chicken salad sandwiches. I loved them, too. Not as much as that first egg salad but damned near. And I had the leftovers from the chicken in the fridge and suddenly this was an omen. I was on a chicken salad sandwich quest. I now understood Marco Polo; he had a spaghetti thing. I sat down on my Sectional with a pen and paper and ran through this in my mind. I'm not completely clueless, so I knew it had celery in it and the chicken was chopped up, and mayonnaise gave it that ooziness. The ones I liked were on white bread and had lettuce fanned out over the chicken mixture. There might have been salt and pepper in there. But that was the problem, I didn't know exactly what was in it and before I destroyed that perfectly good leftover chicken in the fridge, I thought I'd better get some expert advice.

Lots of food turns my crank: french fries, burgers, BLTs. I'm not talking exotic stuff, or anything, I'm talking about stuff you make at home, or at least other mothers make at home. I dug my toes into the silky Quum on the floor and came up with the solution: Google. You can get anything by Googling. Right? Wrong. Turned out a book was the answer. Go figure, eh?

The truth is, I wasn't much for books until that day. As far as I was concerned, books were those things that schools made you carry in your backpack to give you a hunchback. Books weigh a ton. And don't get me started on libraries. Teachers spend hours telling you how to look stuff up in libraries when all you have to do is Google whatever you want and get the answer. "Oh no," they say, "you can never know whether the answer you get in Google or Wikipedia is true." And you say, "well, okay, show us the section in the library where it tells you how to make an atomic bomb at home." And they look at you with real fear on their face and say something like, "you *can't* find *that*!" To which you reply truthfully, "sure you can, I did" and the next thing you know you're in the principal's office and some secret agent from CSIS is dragging your parents into the school. That's how I know how cold these guys can stare at you. And they can do it nonstop for as long as it takes your mother to get all her make-up on and drive down and your father to extricate himself from an extremely important meeting and get the company chauffeur out of his unionized coffee break to drive him up there, too. I think I mentioned that stare earlier.

Sadly, and of course much later, I discovered Google isn't as good as I thought, so maybe my teacher didn't deserve all the ridicule I leveled her way after the atomic bomb CSIS incident. If you Google chicken salad sandwich, you get 327,000 hits, which means probably twice as many recipes as that. I want one recipe, okay? And the ones that come up right on top – and I went through, like, two *dozen* of them – are for six sandwiches when I want one, or ones with walnuts in them, or a dash of sweet pickle relish. First, what the hell is a "dash" and second, I don't think I had sweet pickle relish or even sweet pickles on my chicken salad sandwich. Everyone seems to think whole wheat or pumpernickel bread should be the choice. NO IT'S NOT! I'm pretty sure plain white Wonder Bread is the right choice. And then a lot of them say you should use a food processor to make the thing. I don't think so. My mother doesn't have a food processor but even if she does, it's still in the box somewhere.

After reading these Internet recipes, I came to the conclusion that some people have both the urge and the time to try and reinvent the wheel. Hey, guys, it's ROUND and you can find it ANYWHERE! So with the that first Google failure, I succumbed to the book store idea. If someone is going to go to all the trouble of discovering a recipe and writing it down, and someone else checks it out to see if it's true and then prints it, the thing must be legit, right? And I'll bet you won't find a book with a chicken salad sandwich recipe using "Kraft's French salad dressing" unless Mr. Kraft is the author or it's on the Internet. I think I'm on solid ground here.

I went to one of those huge book store chains. I'm not going to tell you which one because my father says you should always think twice about messing with a monopoly; they tend to "exact Machiavellian pain" if you cross them. I have no idea what he was talking about but it was one of those statements that stays with you. You'll know which book store, though, because you can walk around with a Starbuck's latte while you look around and they have these big chairs, farting chairs, and I'm sure they're built that way, too, because of all the people who sit there for days reading books for free, some of them must fart and the store must not want them to make a noise or smell when they do.

On one wall, over on the side they have this cookbook section and it's huge, right up to the ceiling, and it looks like they have everything, everything except how to make egg or chicken salad sandwiches. It had a sandwich book, all right, but it instructed you to cut the crusts off when you had people over. Yeah, right. Like I'm my mother and this is High Tea. I kept looking. A bunch of chicken books, about a dozen, were grouped together on the shelves but no chicken salad sandwiches. It was as if these authors had collectively decided that chicken, especially leftover chicken, had no value in their gourmet world. Jeezes, sometimes I'm a snob about stuff but these guys were each vying for the Elite Asshole of the Year trophy.

At this point it I began to get curious about the other types of cookbooks and, it turned out, they had all sorts. Vietnamese, Chinese, Thai, American, Italian, French, English (English?), Russian, Ukranian, Polish, Dutch and three Canadian cook books. Then there were the ones I couldn't look at, the *Eat Right & Live Longer* cookbooks." They gave me the chills. I like Chinese so I took one of those and a thin Vietnamese one and also a Thai cookbook to one of the farting chairs and leafed through them, more or less to take a breath and try and figure out how I could have gone so wrong about this book thing. Did you know, for instance, that in Vietnam they have lemon grass? What an invention. You could cut the grass and it would smell like furniture polish at the same time. Cool, but of absolutely no help to me at all. A guy with a name tag walked by a couple of times so I finally stopped him and told him my problem. He took me over to a computer terminal. I should have guessed. A book store with a Googler, the perfect marriage of torture and technology.

Nothing. Not a damn chicken salad cookbook or recipe. Nada. Zilch.

"I probably shouldn't tell you this," he said, "but right down the street a couple of blocks there's a store that sells nothing but cookbooks."

"Yeah, really? What's it called?"

"The Cookbook Store. Never been in it but I pass it every day on the way to work. It's at Yonge and Yorkville. You could try there."

I liked that guy. And it was right where he said it was. I went in and this nice lady asked me what I needed, and when I told her, she went immediately to a shelf and handed me this thing that weighed as much as a brick called *The Joy of Cooking* and you know what? I recognized it. My mother had a ratty old one in her cupboard. Seriously. She had two cookbooks. Only two. This old *Joy of Cooking* with coffee stains on the white hard cover and another called *Home Bistro: creating the best of restaurant cuisine in your kitchen*. I haven't a clue what's in the second one but this one the lady handed me had a recipe for everything. *Everything!* It's a goddamned miracle book. The lady said it was a good way to start, that I should keep it around at all times and I'd never go wrong.

I put it down on a little table in the store and started leafing through it. I didn't even look at the index or anything or the chapters but on some pages it even had measurements. Who knew a tablespoon was worth three teaspoons? You'd automatically think two, right? But nope, it's three. So I bought it right then and there and took it home, opened it up and couldn't believe my luck. I won't lie to you, this thing made Google recipes look sick. But you know what's even sicker? It doesn't have just one recipe for chicken salad, it has suggestions to make different versions but none of them, and I want to emphasize this, none are *wacky*. The thing is, this book gives you classics and variations. You can stray from them but then you'd be entering the Google world of adding salad dressing in chicken salad sandwiches, which I'm pretty sure is wrong. I'm telling you, if someone sold this book door-to-door he'd make fortune. It's that good. Seriously.

So I began to take it to the supermarket. If I saw a piece of meat like a round roast of beef, for instance, I'd look it up and it told me everything I needed to know about it.

Since a round of beef is tough and takes a long time to slow cook (*braising*, is the term: look it up) you can't really eat it like a steak, according to *Joy*. I like steak and I like it rare. I don't like well-done beef, even in stew, which apparently everyone in the world eats all the time. I don't know why, but *Joy* stopped me cold on the *round*, even though it was cheap the day I found it. It's a goddamned miracle book.

The lady in the store told me to get some basics, such as six plates, knives, forks, spoons (big and small) a saucepan, a small frying pan, a measuring cup (and I got a four-cupper because I could use it as a bowl, too). I got them all at the Dollar Store on the way home. Six of everything. I wouldn't have to wash up for almost a week. What a bonus!

It was murder to carry it all home but once I had, I went out to the supermarket and bought celery and bread, mayo and Miracle Whip, because I didn't know which my mother used in her egg salad and I was experimenting, after all. I got a bag of onions, some eggs, threw in some bacon because I love bacon and eggs and BLTs so I also got some tomatoes and lettuce, some instant coffee, milk, and cream. That was even harder to lug back to the house. I fried up some bacon for a BLT and went to toast the bread only to discover a flaw: no toaster. You can't have a BLT on bread. It's just not right. It has to be toast. But I came up with a brilliant idea. I put the slices directly on the burner and flipped them when they got brownish. My smoke alarm works, by the way.

It was at this point of useless back patting that I realized I was stalling, more than a little concerned for my self-esteem given my record with forgers, and took the streetcar to Church Street to see if this Ivan guy really existed.

Church Street isn't that long, about eight main blocks running north and south, three kilometers tops if you don't count the snake tail section north of Bloor, which I don't because there's nothing in that short stretch that interests me. The thing is, you can walk it. Not in winter, of course. Nobody should walk Toronto in winter.

At the top, Bloor Street is the steel beam upon which Church Street hangs, and there everyone dresses like they're going to church or manning a massive funeral parlour. Not surprising, really. St. Paul's Anglican church, one of the city's first, is planted on the south side, and Manulife Financial, an insurance firm once run by Canada's first Prime Minister, Sir John A. Macdonald, looms on the north. And to round out the tableaux of early Toronto, just south on Church itself is Grace Hospital, a small health centre. If you think about it, as I am prone to do to make sense of anything these days, the three of them are like a prelude in a book, or an overture at a musical: life, death and resurrection. I don't know where the political taint fits in there but maybe in all three.

Life starts to pick up slightly after Grace with a few restaurants of high promise on the west side that have not made the optimistic owners rich. You see the neighbouring suits running there at lunch but most of the time, the sidewalk is in no danger of being worn down. It's kind of like a demilitarized zone – barren, grey, unswept – buffering the old Toronto and the Gay Village, a riot of colour a few bocks south that stretches to the old Maple Leaf Gardens. Even if you walk through in the early morning, when everyone is supposed to be asleep, ghost of the night before still float the streets. The place pulses. It bounces like a gangplank. Its rhythm never stops. A high-top symbol sprays a soft beat as the sun comes up over the lake. Then drumsticks start to slap the rim, slowly at first, then faster and louder as the brightly painted buildings throw open the doors and windows in summer and turn up the indoor heat and lights in winter. By evening the rest of the band joins in and the Village is reborn. It's like the place is never more than one day old.

A few years ago a couple of guys and I did a really stupid thing. We were bored, smoked some weed and went down there to 'spot the most outrageous fag.' Really enlightened, eh? What we found was a civilized Carnival, floats of people, mass optimism under a bubble of bands in tune with each other. We were mesmerized by the whole, not the parts, and if anyone, we were the outrageous misfits we thought we'd find. I don't know about the other guys but I felt like a blinded ornithologist; the sport we thought we'd invented was suddenly no longer playable. In the Village, no one hides anymore. They don't need to.

Immediately south of Carlton and Maple Leaf Gardens, Ryerson University sprawls east, west and south, an institution that grinds out the young, some of whom are clear-eyed enough to hope they'll run the city and country one day. Who knows, a small percentage of them might.

Whenever I'm there, I look for me and never find me. I look for Weejuns and see none. Never. I see running shoes, bad ones, but a few good skateboard shoes and the guys who wear them look top-to-bottom put together. Lots of baggy jeans, gum chewing, energy drink chugging, backpack lugging teens and twenties topped by unwashed hair, about 20 per cent of whom are smokers. Cigarettes, that is. I'm never long enough there to get into their personal lives.

A small café right on Church is always packed with Ryerson students. The thing is, they're all colors, shapes and sizes, and very few have obvious accents. Only three, including me, were snowy white when I was there this time. I figured they were all born here, if not in Toronto itself then somewhere in Canada, by the way they added coffee to their mugs of cream and sugar: I didn't need an identity check to figure that one out. It was all very calm and laid back and it occurred to me that if I were an entrepreneur, I wouldn't invest long-term in a chain of high-end tailor shops. Jeezes, I'm sounding like a snob again . . .

Farther south, things turn more practical. The men wear jackets and slacks but no ties, and the women wear very little, even less at night. High-steeple churches on the west side dwarf two-storey pawn shops on the east. You give up your soul on the right, your possessions on the left.

Further south still, the street's namesake, the Anglican cathedral of St. James, is on the east side with a pizza joint on the west side. You can sit at the counter on any given day, eat a greasy pizza slice and watch weddings, funerals and the sobriety of the Establishment of the north end rendered translucent by everyone and everything around them today.

The St. Lawrence Market area dominates the bottom of the street with moderately-priced restaurants, sand-blasted office buildings and a massive barn of an old market building, all under the ugly influence of a crumbling concrete elevated highway funneling people into the city on mornings and shoving them out at night while blocking access to Lake Ontario, the only natural thing within miles. In the barn, and in a low modern brick building across the street, food is sold as agricultural history at prices no farmer, fisherman or wino can afford.

The address the bar lady gave me was in the pawn shop section (duh!) and the store was a narrow grungy place stuck between two way bigger stores, one of which had a sign in the window declaring "we buy gold," the other store loaded with musical instruments, especially trombones, banjos and clarinets. You had to wonder about someone who had to pawn a banjo. I could see the trombone; some kid's father bought it one Christmas because he used to play it in high school and thought maybe his son would be better at it, but all the kid wanted to play was Guitar Hero. But a banjo? That takes asking. You don't just go out and buy your son a banjo. No one has a banjo band in high school. And the one in this window looked good and used, which meant whomever owned it once played it a lot and probably couldn't make a dime and had to sell it. I imagined this guy trying to get down to the Blue Mountains to play a gig and couldn't afford it, and then what does an out-of-work banjo player do? It's not like it's a skill a lot of people want. So it was kind of sad, that window.

The place where Ivan was supposed to be was really dark and narrow by comparison. It looked creepy, so I sort of walked slowly by and looked in. The window was filled with watches displayed in upturned cardboard boxes and a handwritten, felt-pen dollar amount was thrown into each: Everything $20, Everything $30, that kind of thing. Inside the store was lined with jewelry cases. I couldn't see much but a bunch of old cameras in one, and some rings in another. The cases went about three quarters of the way back before another case closed off the back area. I could see myself going in to buy a watch, or maybe a ring, so I didn't feel too intimidated. When I was looking at the cameras, this old guy in a cardigan sweater came down from the back and looked me over. "Can I help?" he asked. It was a kinda rough voice.

"No, no, just browsing," I said. I don't know why but I started to feel heat on my forehead. The guy stood right there looking at me and then shuffled away. "Is Ivan around?" I asked.

"Ivan?" the guy said and turned around to look at me again. "No Ivan here."

"Oh, okay, must have gotten the wrong place then," I said, and started to the front door.

"What's your name?" The voice asked. "It wouldn't be Petra, would it?"

I guess from the expression on my face when I turned around that he got his answer. "Come here," he said, and waved me back into the store.

"Who told you my name was Petra?"

"Petra."

"Yeah, Petra. Who told you that name?"

"Petra did."

"Petra?"

"In Kensington. It's her restaurant. Petra's restaurant. You come with me. I'll take you to Ivan. Don't be afraid, he's not going to bite you. He's expecting you, Petra."

So that's how she picked up on my ID so fast. What are the chances of that? The old guy lifted the right side of the back cabinet and motioned me through. He took me back to a dark little office cluttered with shelves of watches and chains and, well, crap everywhere. At a little desk with one of those jewelers' loops attached to his glasses was a bent-over little guy and he had a cardigan on, too, and not to be unkind, he looked like shit.

"Ivan, meet Petra," the first old guy said. Ivan looked up and gave me a toothy grin, but those teeth weren't real. Nope, those teeth went into a glass with a bubbling Polident tablet beside his bed every night. They looked like they came from a horse's mouth, not from anyone who actually talks. They were huge and yellowy and didn't really have any spaces between them, just indents pretending to be gaps.

"Vell, vell, vell," Ivan said. "Vat do we have here? A young man growing up too slowly?"

"Hi, I'm . . ."

"I know who you are but how do you expect me to help you?"

"ID?"

"Yes, yes, but vat kind? And for what? I can give you new identity completely – passports, citizenship, driving license, birth certificate, credit cards, Health Cards, anything you vant. But a new identity will cost you $20,000. Cash. Somehow, I don't think that's what you vant, no?"

"No. I just want something better than before."

"You mean the Petra license?"

"Yeah, exactly. A new name and address and birth date to show I'm of drinking age. That's all. How much will that cost?"

"So you've thought this through, eh?"

"Well . . ."

"Show me your license now. The real one." I passed it over to him. "See, you don't vant to reinvent da wheel, Petra. All you vant to be is big boy. Give me Health Card. See this," he said, pointing to the address, "why you should memorize new info? Be yourself, Petra, always yourself. See, I make you new licence and card, just change age, one hundred dollar for each year it goes up. You eighteen, you become twenty-one. That way you can drink anywhere, go anywhere, go to Las Vegas!" Ivan laughed. "See, change here, here, here and magnetic strips. Three hundred dollar and you twenty-one. You still same boy, same addresses. If, God forbid, you get into trouble, they phone you daddy or mommy and dey answer the phone, like always, right? No problems. It's how you do it. Be yourself, always be yourself. Okay?"

"Okay," I said. It made sense.

"So you give me three hundred now and come back in two days. It'll be ready. Okay?"

"Okay."

Before I left my place I'd separated bills into my right and left pockets, the left one having five hundred in hundreds, the right pocket twenties totaling two hundred. Before I went down there, I didn't know how much this would cost but I didn't want to go in there flashing too much. I felt into my left pocket and pried out three bills and handed them over. Ivan looked at them in the light and then with his jeweler's loop. "Okie dokie, Petra, two days, you come back."

When I turned to the front, the old guy had already lifted up the counter and was grinning. I made my way down the store to the light and the street beyond. I stood in the doorway, one of those old recessed ones, and thought how great all this was. I mean, in two days I'd be three years older. Poof. It was amazing. I could do anything. I could drink with impunity, I could gamble, I could, could, could, well, I probably could do a lot more if I thought about it but for now, just the feeling of freedom was amazing. I had rid myself of all the stupid social roadblocks devised by politicians who think they're more qualified than me to run my life. Well, screw them. Ivan for Prime Minister!

CHAPTER FIVE

When I woke up the next day I was tired, not in a great way, not like after running fifty laps to watch the entire cheerleading squad practice. That's exhausted but grinning tired. No, this was sort of like someone piped a couple of gallons of water into your veins while you were asleep. When I whirled my legs over the side of the bed they felt heavy. The toothbrush felt heavy, the toast felt heavy and the jam on the toast? Like lead. The thought of eggs and bacon made me want to vomit. Even the voices on *Breakfast Television* came rumbling into my brain on wet string between two empty juice cans. I couldn't remember ever having felt this way. Somebody had strapped two cats to my feet and they were putting their claws into the carpet on the way to the bathroom making my feet scrape along, and then they started to fight when the water got going and I almost fell in the tub. How embarrassing would that be? Eighteen-year-old proves old adage that most fatal accidents happen in the home. He was found with a fractured skull in the bathroom, two cats strapped to his feet.

Did you realize that on a Tuesday morning, there is not a single interesting live sport being played somewhere in the world worthy enough for a basic satellite dish? And there's something just wrong about watching porn at 10:00 a.m., like wearing a tuxedo to breakfast. I thought maybe I'd spend the time planning something. It was either that or stare at some CNN announcer screaming something I don't give a shit about in a 'the-world-is-going-to-end' voice. You ever notice that? These guys are always teetering on their tip toes, or leaning dangerously close to the front of their anchor chairs, brows furrowed, hand wringing, officially certifying a 'breaking news' item that, when you really analyze it, has been broken every few days since King Henry VIII started chopping heads. So planning something was better than that. The casino, maybe.

One of the things I couldn't do was rent a car to get down to Niagara Falls. This proved to be about the only flaw in this plan. I phoned up a couple of places but you had to be 25, apparently, which was a bad thing because it was downright discriminatory, but a good thing because now I was challenged and maybe that would keep my mind off the cats strapped to my feet. I could *buy* a car because the salesman at the *Aston Martin* dealer said if I had the cash, he had the car, and then hung up. But I didn't want to buy one, either, because that would take too long, cost too much, make me an insurance victim and, all in all, piss me off. So I would have to get down to the Niagara Casino some other way. The bus seemed the best and I could go there and back for about $30 if I declared myself as a student, which I was, if I wanted to admit it. So that part was fine. Buses left about every hour during the day. But it left me with no other challenge for the day on the Casino Adventure front. And even though it was now afternoon, porn was still not right. It was mid-afternoon when I heard the aluminum backdoor slam shut and went to the front to see who came out.

The place I rent is on an old street with big trees and no driveways, which necessitates on-street parking, which bureaucratically bestows curbside rights through permits, which cause rational people to commit random acts of violence against cars that don't display said pieces of permit paper on the dashboards. That's not the only defining characteristic of the area. The sidewalks are narrow and become impassible on trash days. I imagine it's the same on snow days, leaf pick-up days, recycling days, garage sale days, and rain days when the catch basins overflow, which pretty well makes them useless. I've seen that.

The house itself is unlike others but only because the houses on either side, with about three feet separating them, are owned by the same guy. He's renovating them so they're empty and noiseless. Each is worth a million bucks or more. If someone comes out the back door of mine, it's either the guy in the basement – The Dungeon Dweller – or the lesbian on the second floor. I have the only front door access making the place look like a single family home, which it is supposed to be, according to the bylaws that no one in the neighborhood pays attention to. The lesbian told me all this the first day I moved in. She came down and barked it all out in a monotone, even the lesbian part, like a demented Welcome Wagon lady, and then left. I've never heard or seen her since even though you can't get out to the street without me knowing because I can see both alleyways from the front window.

This time, a cloaked figure in a grey-felt hat, head down so I couldn't see his face, scuttled down to the sidewalk with his hands in his pockets, feet shuffling like mad, then turned north and disappeared. The Dungeon Dweller. One thing was for sure, he did not look like James Bond. Bond would have been wearing a wrinkle-free trench coat, no hat so all his scars would show, shoes so shiny it would look like the sun was out, which it wasn't, and he'd walk with his head up, beaky nose straight ahead. He might wear gloves because he never lost them like someone else I resemble, and they'd be made of Italian leather. And he would not have walked up the street. Someone would have delivered an *Aston Martin* the second he walked out the door. In fact, he wouldn't have left without knowing the *DBS* was waiting for him. All of which got me to thinking again: If I were going to go the Casino, what should I wear?

Other than the clothes on the floor, my wardrobe was beginning to look a bit thin. A quick check revealed I had one pair of clean underwear in the drawer, two pairs of socks, one brown, one black, a fairly clean pair of pants, and by that I mean they didn't seem to have an oily mayonnaise stain on them somewhere, the blue blazer that never dies because it can go anywhere, anytime, whereas the Harris tweed is a daytime jacket that goes to school or a book publisher's launch in England. And when I thought about that, I thought about the bookstore and the cookbooks and, I now remembered seeing, books on cocktails. Bond would order a cocktail, wouldn't he? He liked martinis but what if he ordered wine, what kind of wine? Boy, this was revealing a gaping hole in my knowledge bank. I was dressed in my Tweed and Weejuns and out the door in a flash, the cats having been shaken off into a corner of my mind.

I went back to the big book store on Bloor, a few blocks west of Church. I took the streetcar ride due east to Yonge Street, the subway north to Bloor, and then walked east. I was then right in the heart of the area where two carats-and-up shop. It's on the north side, tastefully lit up with the other tastefully lit up places with names you see in movies. Tiffany's and Gucci, for instance. My mother used to go down there all the time and a couple of times she took me with her rather than risk me breaking something at home. It was always an education. For one thing, it was here I learned my mother was a serious artist. She'd go into one of these fur coat stores, really long, expensive furs, and she'd study them, go back out to the car and draw what they looked like. Then we'd go down to Spadina where she'd go to this little guy with a measuring tape and he would *buy* my mother's drawing of the fur coat. He actually gave her cash. Not much but how's that for a turnaround? Van Gogh never sold a painting in his *life!* but my mother sold hers within twenty minutes. Not only that but a month or so later, she'd go back down to the little guy and he would have made a coat for my mother that looked *exactly* like the coat in the two-carat zone she drew and it would cost her about a tenth of what it was going for the original. Only one other thing happened when she did this; she would try it on for my father. Every time she did, he would roll his eyes, slap his forehead and walk out of the room shaking his head. Every time. It was uncanny. And my mother would be laughing. The fun was, she said, that *her* coat was made for *her.* It was *definitely not off the rack*, she emphasized, so it would fit no one but her.

"What if you get fat?" I asked. My mother's face was a horror.

"I will *never* get fat," she said. "No one in my family is fat."

"Granny was fat," I said. "She looked like a giant bowling pin."

"That's your granny on your father's side," she said. "She was from Russia and they're all that way. My mother was thin to the end."

"But what if you get fat anyway?"

"I won't!" she said, but then seemed to soften a bit. She took me over to the living room wall and pointed at one of the paintings. "See that?" she said and pointed to a horse charging onto a frozen pond dragging a fat red sleigh with a driver sitting way up and two people on a bench covered by fur blankets from the mid-chest down. The characters were really little but you could, like, see them clearly anyway. That's a sleigh," she said, "in Quebec, and it's really cold and these people have a fur blanket. If I ever get old and fat, which I won't, I'll just use the coats for blankets in winter."

Drink books came in all shapes and sizes at the store so I took four promising-looking ones and sat down in their farting chair to study them. I know it's a little juvenile, but I liked the ones with the glossy pics the best. And the cover said it was the best new drink book in 40 years, "the new definitive work that drinkers everywhere will treasure for life." I spent quite a bit of time with this one and found a recipe for something called a Rusty Nail. Now, that sounded right. Rusty Nail. It sounded dangerous, it didn't have anything in it but booze, also dangerous, and it could go into one of the juice glasses I had at home. I'd try it and if I liked it, the Rusty Nail would be my signature cocktail. On the way out I also picked up a *Wine For Dummies* book because I didn't want to spend a fortune on something I probably wouldn't be drinking a lot. I had to figure out what to buy the inevitable raven-haired Clairol beauty who sat down at the roulette table with me, but I didn't have to be a scholar about the stuff, did I?

I got a little nostalgic on the way out of that book store. Across the street was a furniture store and in the window was an enormous bed that looked like the sleigh in our Krieghoff painting. "Hey Mom!" I yelled, "Look at that! It's that sleigh except it's got no horses. And it's got legs, not runners."

"Yes dear," she said, "that's why it's called a Sleigh Bed."

"Wow, I'd really like one of those," I remember saying, "it's *so big*."

"Well, maybe one day you'll get one," she said, but in that way I knew she was just humoring me.

The memory of that day hit me again when I walked out of the big bookstore. I *had* gotten that sleigh bed. And I remembered that I had made myself a promise to change my mother's mind at the time. I don't know why, but I just stood there looking across the street at the store and started to cry. Just standing there. I couldn't help it, I didn't anticipate it. I must have looked like a complete doorknob, although I don't think anyone saw me. I let the tears roll down my face. I couldn't move. My nose started to run. My lower lip started to shake really fast. Eventually, I shook it off, sucked and swallowed my nose back, wiped what was left on my sleeve and crossed the street to the underground liquor store. The whole thing unnerved me so much that I didn't think twice about going in, grabbing a bottle of Drambuie and a bottle of scotch with a guy in a top hat on the black label, charging right up to the cashier, handing over a wad and then leaving. It didn't occur to me that I didn't have any ID until I was plopping two ice cubes in the juice glass, pouring two teaspoons of Drambuie over the ice, then covering the whole thing with scotch. As I examined my creation, the alarm bells went off. I must have looked so natural the guy didn't even bother asking my age. So was that it? You're grown up when you act grown up? Actual age doesn't matter? Was I, therefore, grown up? Or was I only grown up at that moment, like the reverse, when my mother tells my father to"grow up"? I swirled the drink around and took a swipe. It took my breath away. My eyes teared up, my nose plugged and my breathing stopped. I walked over to the bathroom mirror, swallowed a whole lot of air through my mouth, held the glass up and said, "Bomb, James Bomb." It just came out that way. Bomb. I'd found my signature drink and a secret signature name. But given my previous interrogation, I decided I'd better not use it at the Casino, even as a joke. Those Canadian Security Intelligence guys would not be amused.

CHAPTER SIX

It was "I" Day. Ivan Day. He'd said to come back in two days but I didn't know whether that meant to come back the day after tomorrow at any time, or in a full forty-eight hours. I don't suppose you don't ask guys in Ivan's business something like that. You're just supposed to know. It dawned on me then that I didn't know a lot about Ivan but that he had my *real* driver's licence and Health Card *and* my money. Not only that but it seemed like every newscast on television was about identity theft. What if this Ivan guy stole my identity? I'd really be anonymous then, wouldn't I? But not in a constructive way.

I was never a nervous kid. I never tortured myself with the "what ifs." I never prepared myself for every situation imaginable before I went out of the house, like some people do. If I ran into some problem during the day, I tackled it head on right then and there. This meant I developed a valuable ability to get up to full speed running in the opposite direction in less than a second. But now I was nervous about the Ivan thing. I found myself asking things like, what if I go in there and they just say buzz off? What would I do? What *could* I do. Ivan and his friend were old and all, but they'd probably have guns. They could blow me away and tell the cops I was trying to rob the store and if they planted another gun on my corpse, they could claim self-defense and get away with it. It made me so nervous I wrote a note in my shaky handwriting saying, "To whom it may concern. I was NOT robbing this store, they gunned me down!" and put it in my wallet, folded up but clearly visible for the cops.

Actually I knew why up to then I could go through life tackling problems as they came along because in the end, I could always count on my father to back me up. The problem now was that I still could but I'd be a traitor to my own mission This is when it really became apparent I was on my own. Confidence was having a back-up. No back-up? The time-wasting, emotion-draining, what-ifs must be contemplated, that's what.

How do you get so much confidence that you don't give a shit what happens? As soon as I thought it, I laughed out loud and jumped backwards into the farting chair, clapped my hands and shouted. I'd had another *Holy Cow Moment.* You get confidence when you realize that whatever happens, good or bad, it won't mean jack in a year. Maybe less. And between the good and bad, there's a lot of wiggle room. If all went as advertised, then perfect. If I went into Ivan's and he told me to buzz off, however, I could fight back a little with a few choice verbal threats like I'd ruin his reputation with everyone my age in the city, which I thought was a good one since it would cut into his revenue. And if things got really rough, I could rely on my foot speed and blend in with the university crowd just north if I dressed in jeans, a T, skateboard shoes and a windbreaker, with my backpack over my shoulders. So I did.

Whatever happened, it wouldn't matter in the end. If I got out of this alive.

In less than an hour I was standing across the street looking at Ivan's place, trying to see if there was any life in there. A big black guy with a bulky coat walked in and, a few minutes later, walked out, so it was reasonable to believe Ivan or his assistant were in there. I crossed the street.

I wasn't half way down the centre of the store when I heard his voice. "Petra, Petra. How nice to zee you. Stay dare, I be with you in a zecond." I saw the backdoor was open a bit. I hadn't known about a back door before, but it accounted for the fact that when Ivan got up from his desk, he was in silhouette. When he came into view in the store itself, he was carrying a brown paper bag, which he put on the counter, and then reached in to drag out the contents. Suddenly I was no longer nervous. I took a quick glance at my fingers. They didn't shake. *All the worry for nothing.*

"Here you go, Petra," he said and snapped down two Health Cards and two licences on the glass top. I picked the licences up and compared them; they were identical except for the birth dates. So, too, were the Health Cards. "Ivan does good, no?"

"Christ, yes, you do," I said, marveling at the workmanship. They were even scratched to look used. "These are fantastic."

"Good. You tell all friends Ivan the best, okay?"

"Absolutely," I said. I took off my backpack, opened it up on the counter and put the fake ID into the little side pocket inside. I took the real ones and put them back into my wallet.

I remember more of what happened next than what I said, if I said anything more than I remember, but as soon as I'd stuffed my wallet into the back pocket of my jeans, a huge bang came from the back of the store, loud enough to make both Ivan and I jump. A big guy, Asian, came pounding down to the counter, flipped it up and ran toward the door. He stopped in the entrance, turned and screamed at someone behind us: "They're everywhere!" and then another guy came running through the store, this one looked only slightly bigger than a dwarf. But what then got me was that both of these guys had guns in their hands and they tore outside and headed south. I was about to run to the doorway to see where they went when I heard sirens all over the city, and the pounding footsteps of someone else tearing through the store. As he reached the counter, this guy stopped and looked at Ivan, then me, then back at Ivan.

"You know dis guy?" the man said, gesturing toward me with his head, waving the biggest handgun I'd ever seen. He was huge, black and was wearing that bulky coat.

"Yes, is Petra," Ivan said.

"Goot," the big guy said, and slung a sack of something into my backpack, zipped it up and looked right at me. It scared me. His eyes were more than bloodshot. They looked like little round Jackson Pollock paintings. They were brilliant yellow where the whites should be and cris-crossed with bulging red veins, and in the centre aqua blue irises. I know, I know, but we were members of the Art Gallery of Ontario, so I'd seen a Jackson Pollock before, not that I could see what made him such a supposedly great artist. I'd seen the Andy Warhol exhibit, too, and that one, well, I knew straight off why everyone thought *he* was an artist, and it wasn't the soup cans or the silk screen Marilyn Munroes, it was his movie. Here I was in the esteemed Art Gallery watching gay porn, which is a real turn off, but I got it; art makes you think, or gag, and he'd surely as hell had done that with me. If you showed it outside the gallery, people would burn down the place. But there? It's *art*. So I know what a Jackson Pollack looks like and that's what this guy's eyes looked like, too.

"You bring this back here in two days, got it? Two days, or else," he said, then ran to the front of the store, looked left and right and, like the other two, ran south.

I turned around to Ivan, but all I saw was his back flying out the rear door like a wide receiver, his legs and body feinting right, left, right, before planting his feet and running north. This was so cool! This old guy was running like someone my age and he had to be 90. That's when I started hearing a whole bunch of popping sounds, tires screaming, sirens howling.

I grabbed my backpack to sling it over my shoulder and my arm nearly fell off. Whatever Jackson Pollock had put in there was really really heavy but I slid it from the counter and lugged it to the front. I practically ran right out onto the street, looked south and saw Pollock pointing that gun at me. Me! I saw the gun jolt in his hand, then jolt again, then heard two disturbingly familiar sounds. It sounded like someone was whacking one of those small brown paper lunch bags you take to school as a kid, blow, it up and smack it right behind Heather Winscott's head so she screams and jumps and screams some more and calls you juvenile. I didn't know until way later she wet her pants every time someone scared her, something about a bladder problem. If I'd known that, I might not have done it to her so many times, although, God, it was hilarious. But this wasn't Heather Winscott. This was real, and suddenly what had been so cool was now just scary. I threw myself into the doorway and slid down as far as I could and put my backpack in front of me for protection, but probably just to hide, and watched Pollock blast away with that enormous gun until a cop car came screaming down the sidewalk – the sidewalk, for Christ's sakes – and swung the front left bumper against the shop just south so I couldn't see Pollock anymore, and a cop rolled out of the front seat, gun drawn, pointed it over the hood of the car and started shooting back at him. Then he whirled around and sat down on the sidewalk as he fished out some bullets and started to reload his revolver. That's when he saw me.

"Who the hell are you?" he screamed.

"Did you see that guy? He had a GUN! A fucking GUN! And he was shooting at ME!" I said.

"Don't move," the cop said and turned to stand up again.

"Don't move? Don't move?" I screamed back, "You couldn't get me to MOVE if you tried. That guy had a GUN! I almost SHIT myself!"

The cop pointed his gun down the street again, but he didn't shoot. By now cop cars were screeching all around us. Doors were being opened and slammed shut, people everywhere were yelling "Don't move!"and the cop in front of me turned and said, "You stay there. Don't move until I get back."

"Stay here? Fucking right I'm staying here. Think I want to get shot?!" I said, but as soon as I said it, the cop sprinted around his car and headed south and I couldn't resist getting up. Yeah, I was stupid, but I had to see what was going on. When I looked over the hood of the cruiser, though, I wished I hadn't. Not twelve feet away, Jackson Pollock was lying on the pavement, face down, a black mirror forming around his head.

When I think back on it now, I figure I was pretty rational about the whole thing. I went over and picked up my knapsack, managed to sling slung it over my shoulder and walked slowly but deliberately north on Church toward the university. It was all an instinctual, emotional reaction to a set of facts I had been presented with very quickly. First, I was at the scene. Second, I had a knapsack that I was now certain was full of guns. Third, I had a note saying I did not rob the store, which is like a convicted murderer saying he's innocent even as they pump a lethal dose of drugs into his vein. Right away, I had a lot of explaining to do, the least of which was admitting to the cops I had fake ID from Ivan. And I didn't want to get Ivan in trouble, either. The man was a true artist, after all.

An additional motivator was I wanted to be anonymous and alone, which is why I left home in the first place, and the cops would call my parents right off the bat.

And as I walked away I realized that I had, indeed, shit my pants when Jackson Pollock started shooting at me. Although, I'm fairly sure now he wasn't actually shooting at me, more likely at the cops coming down the street, but it looked like he was trying to kill me at the time.

So I walked north on Church, ducking into a storefront every now and then to see if the cops were coming after me, but they weren't. I knew where I was going, north to Carlton and the streetcar west to my corner, not a long way normally, but when you've shit your pants, you tend to walk the long way around everyone, and even though there are plenty of seats on the streetcar, you can't sit down for obvious reasons, which aren't always obvious to the dozen people sharing the car. It was social agony.

A lot of people were giving me the look, you know, the one that says this guy is a disgusting human being, but they can't quite pinpoint why because no one my age shits himself unless they're completely wacked out on drugs, but I wasn't staggering around like a zombie, except when I had to take off the backpack, which was killing my shoulders. It fell with a clank and scared the shit out of this little Italian widow who recognized the sound of illegal weapons being thrown on the floor. I know, I know, that's such a stereotype but it flashed before my eyes at the time. I'm surprised someone didn't use a cell phone to alert the cops or CSIS that someone suspicious was riding the Carlton/College rails.

The backpack hit the floor inside my front door with the same hell-of-a racket as I tore off my windbreaker and pants on the way to the bathroom. I figured this was going to be ugly. But I was surprised. It felt like a horse patty in my pants but it was just a messy smear. The underwear looked disturbing, though, so I just put them in a plastic bag and threw them out; no way was I going to put those in with the rest of the laundry.

I was in the shower and calmer when I thought about Jackson Pollacks' bounty. I was so concerned about a shit smear in my pants that I just dropped the backpack on the floor. But a gun could've gone off and shot me and how would that look? I would be found dead in the middle of the living room with my pants halfway down and shit in my underwear. I'm pretty sure forensics take photos of crime scenes and show them in court and sometimes on TV. How embarrassing would that be? At least this time no cats would be found strapped to my feet.

I hate guns, really hate them. A couple of friends had been screwing around with a shotgun once and it went off. That was the end of that friendship and I'll never forget the funeral. Another guy I went to camp with went home after one summer and played Russian roulette in his parent's basement and lost. I remember going numb head to toe when I heard about it. But the worst was something I did.

I'd learned all about guns at camp and I became the youngest gold CIL sharpshooter in camp history. We only shot 22s but still, they can kill you just as fast as a shotgun. I was a kid, though, and death wasn't on the radar. They taught us how to shoot, warned us that you never pointed at anyone or anything you didn't intend to kill, which was a very scary thought then and, since Jackson Pollack, now, too.

The worst sin you could do at camp, however, was smoke a cigarette. Cigarettes would kill you. No question. No reprieve. So when we caught Saul Shloman sneaking one behind the Kaibah, which was the outdoor can, we hauled him up to the shooting range, stood him standing sideways beside target Number One and I aimed and shot a cigarette straight out of his mouth.

Twenty-twos don't go "pop," like a big handgun, as I found out outside Ivan's place, they go "crack." One "crack" and Saul was crying, screaming and running: "Get away from me! Get away from me! You could have killed me!" he yelled. We laughed like hell. I've gotta say though, at that point we knew we'd be thrown out if the camp director found out and that would mean a whole lot of explaining to the parental units.

We found out later from his tent mate that he was screaming when he got back to his bed but he was screaming he'd never smoke again, not that he was going to get us if it took him the rest of his life. Which was a relief. I still don't know why Saul didn't say anything to anyone else. He'd have had us by the balls.

The next day the wind was howling in from Little Lake, really blowing hard, and we were joking we would be rolled right off the shooting platform. I took aim, fired and missed the target completely. I had never, ever failed to hit a bull's-eye. I shot again and this time I saw a little spray of dirt splash up to the right of the straw, which served as the backstop. This was alarming and I hoped nobody noticed, so I aimed way left and fired another round. I hit the target, left of the bull's-eye, but I hit it. I checked the sights. Nothing wrong. And then it hit me. The wind.

I looked up, spotted where I had to aim to hit the target, mentally made a calculation as to how far right the bullet had been pushed and, with a gut-cramping feeling, realized I would have hit Saul in the back part of his jaw if I'd shot at that cigarette that windy day. I dismantled the rifle, packed up and left. I never shot a gun again.

On the last day of camp I went over and gave Saul a big hug. That must have really scrambled his brain. We had never hit it off. Saul was a complete nerd, way worse than me, and I hugged him. He looked at me like someone had just rammed a broomstick up his ass and he a) couldn't believe it and b) it took his breath away it hurt so much. He was still bugeyed when he got into his parents' station wagon and drove off.

I didn't know what I'd do with all the guns Pollock had given me. They would have been hot, probably used in all sorts of criminal activities, maybe even a murder or two, and I would either have to give them to the cops or. . . or . . . *Jeezes* I didn't know. You couldn't just toss them in the garbage. The bag might break. You see that on TV all the time.

I didn't bother picking the backpack off the floor, just unzipped it, pulled out the bag Pollock stuffed in, pulled the drawstring and tipped it up from the other end. It made a hell of a racket, a zillion metal things, each twice as wide but half as long as a stick of gum. All gold. Seventy-six one-ounce gold wafers. Four and three quarter pounds of gold. I picked them up, fingered them, weighed them in the palm of my hand, felt how smooth they were, read the little numbers punched into them, licked a couple to see what they tasted like, dropped one on the floor to hear if it clanged or went thump (more of a thump), spun it around to see if it wobbled.

According to a Google, they were worth roughly $75,000 on the market that day. A big, shiny pile of gold. I stacked them up and made a little log cabin with them and then just left it all in the middle of the floor. I sat down in my farting chair and just stared at it.

Know what happens when $75,000 drops into your lap? Paranoia and shear terror. An acute sense of hearing; every creak in the floor is a crack of an assault rifle pointed your way, every siren is a police car racing to your house to bust down the door to arrest you for gold theft, every drunk cursing outside at night is some friend of Pollack whispering orders to a his gang to wait until you appear at the window before firing and then collecting the lost loot.

It's not fair. Someone hands you a new life with a new ID and $75,000 and you're trapped inside the house for the rest of your life for fear of being abducted, jailed or killed, the three biggies in Paranoia Land. All you want to do is go down to the Casino and act like James Bomb and you can't because either the cops or the friends of some dude with goofy eyes are after you.

I sat on the can, rubbing my temples, thinking about the whole wretched deal but my mind kept getting messed up with what had happened, and then flipping over mid way to what would happen as a result of what happened, then flipping again to what I could have done, and then what was I going to do now? About what? Shit, I'd start all over again except it wouldn't go in a straight line through what I had already thought about. So I'd start again. It didn't help. I'd stop whenever I came across something I didn't know but probably should, like what happened to the two other guys who ran through the shop? And why did Ivan run? And what happened to him? And the other old guy? And then the most important question of all: What about ME? I knew about me in the whole scheme of things, but did the cops? I mean, one cop saw me but did he know I was in the shop and saw everything? Were they looking for me? As a witness? As an accomplice? I practically ran to the TV.

TV is not Google. You have to wait, like years, to get the story you want. In this case, it was on the five o'clock local newscast, right at the beginning. I damned near missed it as I remoted through the channels. But there it was on the tube, a few seconds into the story, video showing just south of Ivan's place, cop cars on the sidewalks, Jackson Pollock under a tarp or a blanket or something. The announcer said what time it all happened. She said one suspect was shot dead outside the store, two other men had been caught nearby, one was dead and the other in hospital with life-threatening injuries after a shootout in an alley behind the jewelry store where an unidentified amount of money had been taken. "It was gold, you idiots! Gold!" I yelled at the screen. And then the announcer said the owner of a pawn shop next door and his employee were also shot dead.

"Oh, God, no." Those three words just leaked out my mouth like they had been packaged eons ago and put somewhere in my brain to be ejected like that when something absolutely terrible happened. It made me feel empty, like a punctured tire maybe. I stopped thinking. My hands got really cold, really fast. I started shivering. Ivan. Ivan was dead. The other old guy was dead. I didn't know Ivan. I'd met him only twice but for some reason, while Jackson Pollack and his friends were merely crime statistics, Ivan felt like a personal loss. Oh, the other old guy, too, but this was more about Ivan. A little old guy hunched over a dingy desk at the back of a dark office like a little old grandfather as if he'd crack if you touched him. And then the sight of him running out the back door. Could I have actually seen that? Was the whole scene playing tricks on me? It was amazing. But he was *alive*, really *alive*, zigzagging like an Olympian. And then dead. And his friend, too.

It's awful when people die but in cases where more than one person bites it, do your feelings concentrate more on one of them than the others? A big-time athlete dies in a private plane crash with "along with his assistant," as if the assistant was just collateral damage. They almost seem reluctant to mention the pilot and crew. This time the news reduced Ivan to collateral damage and I reduced his friend to collateral damage.

I'll bet the family of the collaterally-damaged feel doubly shitty when they read the papers or watch television.

I didn't hear another thing the announcer was saying. The TV was garbling and hissing static after she had pronounced him dead. I left it that way and found myself curled up on top of my sleigh bed. I don't know how much Ivan weighed, but I'll bet not more than 150 pounds. A bullet weighs what, an ounce? And 150 pounds is how many ounces? I tried to do the math in my head. It took about seven tries and by then I'd come up with either twenty-four thousand or two thousand four hundred ounces but whatever, it was a lot. So on the one hand you have this twenty-four hundred ounces arranged in such a way that it can walk and talk and create great art, and a single ounce injected into it, is fatal. Think about it. It sure as hell doesn't take much to end it all.

I pulled the top blanket over me and closed my eyes. That's when I began to think that Pho might have been onto something. If true, this whole predicament was going to seriously limit my time.

I felt like puking. Really. My stomach was all knotted up and a dull ache was forming just above my bellybutton, just like it did when I was a kid, just before I hurled a gallon of fresh apple cider. Now I was so worked up, clutching my stomach, my mouth flooding with spit, I ran hunched over to the bathroom and sat down on the can so I could whirl around and puke if I had to. I sat and rocked. I thought I'd burst into tears. And then I thought, why not? I was alone. No one could see me. I was being gypped and I couldn't do a damned thing about it. So I rubbed my head like I was shampooing my hair, and started to cry. Then that gypped feeling just started rolling its way down my entire body sucking the strength out of everything. It took over and when I let it, my shoulders bobbed up and down and I actually remember letting out a little wail.

I have no idea how long this actually went on but it was quite awhile, long enough that I dried right up and my ass hurt from sitting on the can so long. I was cold so I wrapped one of the big bath towels around my shoulders, sat in the farting chair and rocked like a retard thinking about why I couldn't control this crying stuff. It was just sort of taking over.

I don't know if you'd call it being weak or suddenly sentimental but I realized that I'd started feeling out of control even before I came out of the bookstore and looked across the street at the sleigh bed furniture store. When I first moved in, I was looking out the front window as the sun was going down and the tops of some of the trees were lit up while others weren't and the leaves and trunks farther down got progressively more brown then dark grey near the ground as the sun sank lower. But the very tops of those trees, as they waved in the wind, were brilliant and they made me think about some of the paintings I'd see in the Art Gallery of Ontario, the old English ones especially, and I remembered someone saying painting and photography were all about light. So I looked even harder. Then I thought about actually painting what I was seeing and as I thought, I realized what a huge job it would be, but what a huge sense of satisfaction artists must feel when they've done it. And my eyes started to sting so badly they filled up. I put it down to being tired, to being so happy about the new place, to be witnessing beauty that I had never noticed before. I shook it off and turned on the TV and sat there staring at God knows what. But now, as I sat there on the floor playing with the wafers, I knew it wasn't a one-off thing. This involuntary crying was probably going to stay with me. The black sludge couldn't be washed off with soap and water. I figured it had to dry and then be chipped off with a chisel.

I played with the wafers until I figured, what the hell, if the cops were coming for me, I'd flat out lie. Shit, Pho might be right and if that were the case, I didn't have enough time left to wait until the judicial paperwork cleared me of anything but shitting my pants.

But I'd have to hide the wafers.

Do you know how hard it is to hide that many gold wafers? They may be small but they're heavy. You can't put them in a magazine, they just fall out with a clank. I don't have a library so I can't put them in books. Even the *Joy of Cooking* won't take more than one, and it's a big fat book. Sock drawer? First place the cops would look. Under the mattress? Ditto. But under the bed frame? Who'd look there, right? So I took the sleigh bed apart and lined the rails with the wafers and then, with considerable effort, which took damn near three hours to get it right without the little buggers clanking to the floor every time I tried to put the frame back on, I had a bed worth way more than $80,000 when you figure in the wafers, the bed, the mattress, the delivery guys . . . And guess what? The way I put them in there, well, it straightened out the mattress frame and it no longer went thump when I jumped up and down. Bonus! It really lifted my mood for a bit. Everything has its purpose in life, right? Nothing is random. That's what I was thinking when I jumped into bed and thought about an $80,000 night in a thumpless bed. Other than the Queen, I figured I was sleeping on the most expensive bed in the entire world. Except I couldn't. Sleep, that is. The feeling that the cops had surrounded my place and were about to crash through the front door came back as the sun disappeared and the street lights came on. So I got a couple of blankets, a pillow and got under my bed. They might not find me there. Why would anyone with a bed like mine asleep *under* it? Even the cops would see that and leave empty-handed. When I woke up, the sun was halfway across the sky.

CHAPTER SEVEN

In everybody's life there comes a time when you have to say, "Screw them if they can't take a joke." When I slid out from under the bed I did not feel like crying any more. I felt like putting my fist through someone's face, although whose face I didn't know and I've never actually punched anyone in my life. I had the feeling I'd just been screwed out of some time and damned if I had any to spare. I woke up with my fists clenched, teeth grinding and said to the mirror, "Screw them if they can't take a joke!" It made absolutely no sense then or now but there it was, hanging in the air.

Because of some bastard with Pollocky eyes, part of my life was completely out of control. Know what that means? I do. It means part of your life is trapped in the future. Your life now becomes pure speculation. It's theoretical. You worry about what might happen as a result of something that happened in the past, and it's doubly frustrating if you had nothing to do with whatever happened. Like me. You can spend you time preparing for the shit to hit the fan at some point or you can ignore it and resolve to confront the problem if it ever surfaces. For me it was simple. The night before my life was speculative. When I woke up screaming, "Screw them!" it was back in the right direction — full speed and damn the torpedoes.

I had the last piece of pure art Ivan was ever going to produce and I wasn't going to waste it. I was going to the Casino and I wasn't going near the bus station. I'd take a cab. Hell, if I could afford to go to a Casino, I could afford a cab, right? I was going with my head high and take whatever came my way, cops or no cops.

Although, truth be told, I put the phony ID in my wallet, grabbed a couple of gold wafers I hadn't been able to fit under the bed frame, snuck around the back and jumped three fences before getting to College Street two blocks south. No use being completely obvious about it.

I flagged down the first taxi I saw. "To Fallsview Casino," I said, in my best Bomb voice, full of confidence, a little world-weary. The driver turned around in his seat and looked at me with crinkly eyes like I was a living practical joke.

"You know how much that cost?" he asked.

"Well, not exactly, but I'm good for it," I said.

"Two hundred sixty five dollars," he said. I had already taken out a wad of bills from my pocket to impress him. The price took my breath away but I'd already made my move, my claim, that I was "good for it," even though it broke a sweat on my forehead. He was calling my bluff. I was in a high stakes game here and I wasn't even at the Casino. I couldn't lose this one, could I?

"How old are you?" the driver asked. I thought that was a little personal.

"Twenty-one," I said.

"Why do you not just take you to the shuttle downtown?" he said.

"Why?"

"Because the shuttle costs $35."

A shuttle? A shuttle? I pictured a bus load of old guys, raisins, drooling and snoring for about two hours, each and everyone of them calling me "sonny," with the little old ladies barely restraining themselves from hugging me and saying "you seem like such a nice young man" until I either puked on them or killed them with my bare hands, not that I've killed anyone with my bare hands, or anything. I haven't even punched someone. I think I already told you that.

"No, no, it's all right. And besides, I like your cab."

"You like my cab?"

"Yeah, it's comfortable, sort of."

"Sort of?"

"Yeah, what kind it is?"

"It is a Chevrolet."

"Really! I've never been in a Chevy before."

"You have never been in a Chevy? A Chevrolet?"

"Nope. Never. It's okay."

"What have you been in, if you have never been in a Chevy?" he said, pulling out from the curb, heading west and then south to the expressway.

"Oh, don't get me wrong, I've been in domestic cars once in awhile, just never a Chevrolet, so this is new. I've been in General Motor's cars, Cadillacs and a Hummer or two. I was once in an old Chrysler Imperial, I think it was called. It had these deep cloth seats that were molded, carved, a bit like an Aubusson carpet."

"An Aubusson carpet? You know about Aubusson carpets?"

"Oh yeah, we have them at home, you know, for the boots and stuff in winter."

"You are kidding me, right?"

I wasn't. I didn't know where he was coming from and decided I shouldn't get into any farther. "Yeah, an Imperial," I said, "nice car. Was smooth, too, a bit clunky maybe but fairly stable in the sway area. Like this one. And I've got a friend who has a Viper. I've been in Ford-built cars, Lincoln Town Cars, a Continental, Fords like that. It's funny, eh? I've spent my whole life and never been in a Chevrolet."

"Really," he said, "and what do your parents drive then?"

"They lean toward British cars," I said. "My mother has this old Jag. My father tells her to get something else, something newer because it's an old Jag and as soon as it snows, you can't go anywhere in it. It just sits there in the snow and spins its wheels, so my mother spends a fortune getting a driver to get her around in winter. My father wants her to get a new car but my mother heard they were being made by Ford and she won't have a Ford."

"What a conundrum," the cabby said.

"You're right there," I said. "My father, he drives a tank. It'll go anywhere."

"A tank?"

"Yeah, that's what I call it because it's so bloody big and heavy. Luckily it's got a 5,000 horsepower engine in it."

"Five thousand?"

"Okay, okay, that's an exaggeration, but it's a big engine so you don't know it's such a huge car."

"What kind?" The cabby was looking at me through the rear view mirror.

"A Bentley."

"Ah, a Bentley. So your father is a prince or something?"

"Nah, just a regular guy," I said, then saw the cabby's picture in a sleeve taped up to the back of his seat. "Your name really Abdul?" As soon as I said it, I knew I'd entered the dark end of social *faux pas*. He looked at me though the mirror again. His eyes were a bit narrower.

"Yes," he said. His voice trailed off and went silent, like he was flushing and studying the toilet to make sure the twister was sucking everything down correctly.

"No, no, that's good. It doesn't matter to me. Good name that. Where are you from?" I was trying to be nonchalant now.

"Toronto," he said.

"No, I mean, like, originally."

"Toronto," he said.

"Oh, sure, yeah, okay. I didn't mean anything by it. I was just curious."

The eyes were studying me again. "My family is originally from Iran," he said.

"Cool," I said, and then shut up. The way I was going, this guy was going to stop the cab in the middle of nowhere, take my money and leave me at the side of the road for being racist. I wasn't racist. Not a racist bone in my body. Some of my best friends are racists, but I don't give a shit whether someone is from Iran, Japan, Costa Rica or Mexico. Well, Mexico's a bit dicey from what I'd heard. I mean, I liked the idea of crossing the border at Tijuana and getting laid for 50 cents, and that's where Caesar Salad was invented, but a Third World country right on the border like that, it's creepy. You'd think something like democracy or affluence would rub off on them. So Mexico was a question mark with me. But only that.

I looked out the window and we were on this high bridge over a bay. To the right were these great grey smokestacks spewing fire and steam into the air and a cloud of it trailed south like a huge squirrel's tail. The Chevy was comfortable and smooth but I was starting to get queasy so I just closed my eyes and let my head fall back on the headrest, and I must have fallen asleep because I had all these weird dreams of traveling on trains and planes and not being able to wake up and missing my destination and getting lost. When I woke up, we were traveling beside neat rows of grape vines.

"You fell asleep," Abdul said. "You talk in your sleep, you know. Like my oldest son. He talks, too."

I adjusted my eyes to the light. My chin was wet. I had been drooling. I hate drooling. It's so pathetic. I wiped my chin with the back of my hand and then dragged it across my shirt, and then realized what I'd done, compounding my idiocy. "You have children?" I said. "How many?"

"Six," he said.

"Six, eh? What ages?"

"Twelve is the oldest, the sleep talker. Two is the youngest. Two, four, six, eight, ten and twelve."

"Every two years, like clockwork," I said. He saw my smile.

"We go back to the old country to see my family every two years."

"Ah, I see," I said, not seeing at all, really.

"What's your family do in Iran?"

"They are jewelers."

"They make jewelry?"

"That is what they do, yes."

"Why aren't you a jeweler, too?"

"I am."

Now I was confused. I guess it showed because he was giving me the eye in the mirror again. "My family, we have a small shop, but gold, the price of gold is very high now. When we came, it was about three hundred dollars an ounce, three fifty sometimes. But now, it is more than seven or eight hundred and my customers, they can get their jewelry back in the old country for less than I can make it here, so I cannot afford to buy it without another income, so I have this cab and it helps."

"Gold, eh?" I said. My mind was going like crazy. "What do you do with gold?"

"Buy it, melt it down, make rings and necklaces and other fine pieces."

"Melt it down?"

"Sure, you get a small smelter."

"And you know what to look for in gold, right? I mean, you can tell if it's good, right?"

"Of course."

I fished out a wafer and handed it over. "This what you use?"

I wish I'd had a camera to record the guy's eyes when he looked at it and turned it over in his hand two or three times, put it in his palm and hefted it up and down. "If you do not mind," he said, "Where did you get this?"

I hadn't anticipated that question. I couldn't very well say Jackson Pollock stuffed it into my backpack just before the cops gunned him down. "My grandmother gave it to me," I said. I am a god damned genius when I have to be. Who else would give you a gold wafer if not for a grandmother? Not mine, of course. All she gave me was bad advice, like, "if you're going to smoke, be a real man and smoke Camels without a filter." But the vision of a grandmother giving you something, well, it *could* be a gold wafer, couldn't it? Your parents wouldn't give you one, they'd give you cash or a credit card, not gold. But a filthy rich granny? Sure. "She gives me one of these every Christmas, every birthday. Has for years. Don't know what the hell to do with them, though, so I thought I'd take some down to the Casino. It's like found money, no? Except I don't know if they're actually going to cash one of these. You're in the business, where should I take this thing?" I asked, and stretched my hand across the seat to recover the wafer. He handed it back to me.

"To a jeweler," he said.

"But *you* are a jeweler. Why don't you buy it from me?"

"Like I said, it is too expensive for me."

"So, you know anyone who would buy it?"

"Maybe for a small price."

"Okay, how small?"

"I do not know. Do you want me to find out?"

"Sure," I said, and thought he'd give me his phone number when the ride was over and tell me to call him later, only he wouldn't give me his real number and I'd be left hanging. I don't know why I thought that. It was kind of presumptuous, but that's what I thought at the time. Abdul, however, surprised me. He picked up his cell phone, dialed and started speaking gibberish, probably Iranian. He went on like this for about two miles, maybe more, and was writing stuff down as he drove. That kind of worried me but it turned out all right.

"Okay," he said, "I got a place. A friend of my cousin, he owns a jewelry store in Niagara Falls. He has agreed to take a look and buy if it is good. It is good, though. I know. You are going to be fine. Just a matter of a discount."

"Discount?"

"Well, yes, discount. The amount he is going to take off the top for the convenience. But do not worry, he's a friend of my cousin and my cousin, well, you do not want to fool around on him."

Truth is, he could take a whack of "discount" off the top and I wouldn't have cared. I just wished I'd brought more of the suckers. This was turning out well so I sat back and enjoyed the view, which came to an end just after another big bridge, but that, as it turned out, wasn't far from The Falls.

Abdul had obviously been given directions to the jewelry store on the phone because he drove right to it. He stopped the cab in front of a little one-storey square wooden house and announced our arrival. I looked out and got the creeps; it looked a hell of a lot like Ivan's place on Church Street but rickety. I was about to baulk when Abdul jumped out, came around the car and opened the back door. It wasn't so much of an invitation to get out as an order, the way he ripped the door open and reached in to help me out. For a second, I thought, okay, this is it, I'm going to get mugged, or worse, but when we went in, an old man with a huge hook nose and glasses perched on the end greeted us with a wide toothy smile and shook my hand. His hand was warm and dry and friendly, like he knew me. Abdul and this guy started with the gibberish and the next thing I knew I was handing over not just one of the wafers but both of them.

"It is a good deal," Abdul told me. "The going rate is $800 an ounce. He will take it off your hands for $650 each."

The last time I looked on Google it was $880 an ounce but the idea of $1,300 cash in my pocket, the Casino around the corner, and a supermodel on my, arm made my head spin a little. If I felt weak in the cab because I was sick, I was dizzy now with my good luck. I held out my hand and the old guy counted out thirteen one hundred dollar bills. I'd never had that much cash in my hand. Sure, my mother's credit cards were worth way more than that but, seriously, this was cash. Cash. Who knew you could run around with that much cash these days?

I thought we were about to leave so I gave him a bigger smile than I thought was seemly but the old guy ushered us to the back of the shop, which was just as messy as Ivan's place, and handed me a cup of what Abdul called tea. This was all well and good but this wasn't something served at The Windsor Arms or the King Eddy hotels in the afternoon with scones and jam. This was teeth-cracking, sweet, oil-slicked water and it made both Abdul and this old guy cackle through what I now saw as crooked walnut-stained teeth. Hideous, really. A bit frightening and it must have shown because Abdul got up, said something in whatever language that was, shook hands with the old guy (and so did I) and we went back to the cab.

"So what are you going to do after you drop me off at the Casino?" I asked.

"Go home, I suppose," said Abdul, "unless you want a driver for the day."

"A driver?"

"Sure. I will take you to the Casino and sit outside. That way you can come and go whenever you want. Say you want to see The Falls. You come out, I drive you there and drive you back. Or to a restaurant. If I am not there, you will grab a local taxi and it will cost you and you will have to wait. But now you have the money, why not have your own ride whenever you want it? And when you want to go back home, I will be here to take you back and you will not have to pay a local cab a fee that could cost more than mine."

All this sounded like a damned fine idea in theory, "but how much is this going to cost me?"

"Well, let us see," he said. "If I take you back now, it is another $265, and then I would spend maybe another three hours driving around Toronto and maybe make another $200, so I would charge you that, but no more."

"So that'd be seven hundred and thirty . . ."

"And maybe a tip, if you like the service."

"And even if I don't, right?"

He smiled through the mirror again.

"Okay, so another hundred. That fair?"

"Sure," he said, and shrugged a little.

"Now we're up to eight hundred and thirty. Let's round it out to eight hundred and fifty."

"If you like."

I thought about it for about as long as it took Jackson Pollock to stuff my backpack. "Okay, you got a deal," I said, just as he drove up to the Casino entrance and turned around in his seat. "I suppose you want to be paid now."

"Only for the ride down plus another hundred to wait around."

"How will I get you to meet me here?"

"Here is my cell phone number. Just call. I will be two, three, five minutes away, at most."

What would I be risking, a hundred? Sounded good to me, so I gave him four hundred, took the cell number and put it in my wallet, shook his hand, said thanks, and waved goodbye and he squealed out of there. And sure enough, as soon as I walked in, a rent-a-cop stopped me and asked for ID. I've never felt more confident than that in my life. Good old Ivan. Good old jewelry guy. Good old Abdul. I had arrived.

CHAPTER EIGHT

The first thing you notice about a Casino are the lights. Blazing. Flashing. Then the noise. Bells are ringing all around you. If there's an energy crisis, it certainly isn't in this place. Everything is moving. Nothing is standing still. Lights whirl around slot machines, people's arms pump up and down on levers, and when they're not, they're push buttons to make the tumblers spin. Every now and then heavy tokens fall into metal slots and more bells go off.

You'd think the little old ladies with the thin nightie-like flowery dresses would have forearms like sailors as they dominated four or five slot machines at a time, moving between them like fleet commanders pulling torpedo levers in an ecstasy of the annihilation of all enemies imagined or real. But Casinos don't cure skin flaps or encourage self-analysis.

Deeper into the room are the table games, the James Bomb area, where people sit around green felt tables staring at cards in their hand, or peeling back the corners of two or three lying flat on the surface in front of them. Scattered around are the Roulette tables where chips are slapped down on squares and lines before the guy who whips a Ball Bearing onto the wheel waves his hand to stop the betting. He's got style. His hand flies low over the table like a magician sweeping his cane over an Opera hat. The rabbit in the hat can breathe, of course, but the gamblers who can't afford to be there don't until the ball drops.

I didn't know what the hell was going on but I thought it would be good if I just watched a bit before I played anything, just to get the hang of things, and that's when I noticed you couldn't sit down anywhere and just watch the action. You had to stand. And when you just stood there, guys in black suits would stare at you like you were some kind of terrorist, ready to pounce as soon as they saw a battery wire sticking out your fly. They were about the only people just standing around and not moving anything but their heads. Beneath the suits they seemed coiled like springs in a cheap sofa ready to shoot up and puncture your sphincter if you moved your hands beneath the seats to find some change. I was getting a bit antsy about this when I spotted a little bar on one wall.

"What'll you have?" the barman said.

"A Rusty Nail, please." I didn't look directly at him. Frankly, I was afraid he would burst out laughing and have me carted out in a huge garbage truck.

"Sure," he said, "you've got some ID?"

As casually as I could, I handed him the Ivan ID, still not looking at him.

"Premium or regular," he said. He seemed to sneer at the regular reference.

"Premium," I said.

"Anything in particular?" he asked. I knew it was a trick.

I looked up at him and fixed him with a steely gaze, desperately trying to remember what I had at home: "Johnny Walker Black."

"Very good, sir," he said, but he didn't say "sir" in the condescending way the Mobilia Shoppe guy said it, and he didn't say it like he was forced to say it, he said it like he said it whenever he recognized a "sir" as opposed to a kid, or a boy or a nuisance. I liked him.

"First time?" the barman asked.

"Oh, no, I drink these all the time," I said, raising the glass and taking a sip. I thought I was going to choke and spit it all over this guy's face and jacket. He didn't make it the same way I did; it wasn't nearly as sweet. I know my eyes went wide and watery. My throat felt like I'd eaten deodorant. You've tried that, right? Take a lick of *Speed Stick*? Your tongue instantly goes dry. It feels like another organ entirely and no matter how many times you try and lick the top of your mouth to get some moisture back, it doesn't work. Actually, now the top of your mouth is bone dry and if you move your tongue anymore, your whole mouth is going to dry up and you'll die just as if you are in the Foreign

Legion trapped in the desert until the buzzards circle and pick your carcass clean. Really. It's awful. And we put that under our arms every day after a shower. What *are* we thinking?

"No, I mean, first time at the Casino," the barman said. I nodded. I couldn't say anything. The barman looked over my shoulder and waved someone over. "This is our Pit Boss," he said. "If you've got any questions, just ask him, he'll tell you. He'll even show you how to play to win."

I looked at the Pit Boss through tears. He had this kind smile, not a stupid smile, or a pitying smile, a really nice smile. I trusted him. I trusted the barman, too. Really. Trusting someone who works for the Casino in a Casino, what a bizarre concept. Except the Pit Boss was a terrific guy. He took me around to the tables and explained to me what was going on, how if you played all the corners and lines on the roulette table instead of plunking down a wad on one number, you could actually make a small profit, like 10 per cent, he said, "and 10 per cent is a good return on your money." And then we watched some Black Jack and he told me at what point you want to stop asking to be hit because the odds begin to go against the dealer. He told me all about Texas hold-em poker, which I'd see on TV, except this Casino didn't play the same game exactly, but one that was very similar, and he gave me this card with all the winning hands on it and odds of those hands. The barman was right. This guy was gold. And sure enough, I played roulette and I never played once where I came up empty. Sometimes I didn't get back all my chips and eventually had to buy a few more, but at one point I was a hundred up and the Pit Boss nodded that maybe I should walk away a winner. I did.

Next I tried the Black Jack table. It was a lot less work, a lot simpler and just as much fun. In fact, when I lost and laughed, everyone at the table laughed with me and the others, at times, told me what I was doing wrong, as did the guy who was dealing the cards. After awhile, I was up about ten bucks, figured I had spent about five bucks an hour and I'd had a great time. Go to a two-hour movie, get some popcorn and a drink and you'd spend more than twice as much. So really, they're ripping kids off while adults have way more fun for less.

So I left that table and was about to go over to the poker table but thought maybe it was lunch time, or maybe a bit later than that. I don't wear a watch and you know what? Neither do any of the people working there and I couldn't see a clock on any wall. In fact, I couldn't see outside from anywhere to see what the sun was doing. So I trusted my stomach that it was lunch time and wandered through the Casino looking for a restaurant.

Up near the ceiling all around the place were these road signs, you know, the ones you see in the movie comedies telling you that New York is 5,500 miles away, Paris is 3,000 miles, Nevada is . . . Well, you get the idea. But these signs had names on them I didn't really know about, but were all pointing at the sides of the huge room, so I went around the outside and, sure enough, there were restaurant entrances every now and again. Most were these cafeteria-style places where some sadist withers discount food under heat lamps but lineups snaked around the corners at these places like they were amusement rides. At least they sold it for what the food was worth, just about nothing.

Eventually I found a place where a guy in a suit actually stood behind one of those maître d' stands and, after looking me up and down from my shoes to my shirt collar, led me to a table by a window that looked out on what I realized was Niagara Falls way below. I had this queasy feeling that it was just there to tease me. I looked through the dining room to the entrance door and, although I couldn't see the games, I could imagine the lights and the bells and the white noise of the casino proper, and everyone in there looking down at tables or straight ahead at the whirling tumblers, duped into a catatonic state by preposterous hope. And then I looked back at The Falls, a magnificent, effortlessly powerful force of beauty that purred It struck me as being like a prisoner clutching the bars and looking down at a brothel. I thought about this piteous scene for a few minutes and then figured, *screw them if they can't take a joke,'* and started to plan for the afternoon's assault on the Casino's vault.

I decided upon a hit and run. I'd get a bucket of coins and chips at the wickets. Then I'd start walking in circles from the outside in and play everything, but never more than a couple of times at one place, and finish at the Black Jack tables in the dead centre. It was a good plan and I was getting excited at the endless possibilities of fame and fortune. I called for the bill. The steak wasn't as good as the view but somehow it had symmetry; the price was so high it would make the sane run to the edge, and jump over.

Bucket of coins in hand, I watched a nightie-clad septuagenarian repeatedly jiggle her underarm fat by throwing in three $1 coins at a time and pulling the lever like she was pulling the switch on the electric chair. She slugged three more coins into the slot before the tumblers had even stopped. A little old man beside her was held together by a pair of blackish pants pulled up to his chest and held there by a cracked brown leather belt from the Second World War. He didn't waste energy with the lever, he carefully put three coins into the slot and then punched a button with the meat of his fist. And unlike the lady, he unblinkingly watched the tumblers stop. I thought if he won, he'd never blink, just keel over right there and die from shock.

These two guys looked like pros so I sat on one of the cushiest stools you can imagine at a slot just past them and put three coins in and pulled the lever. It was more fun than punching a button, I figured. These tumblers spun around and stopped. The whole machine began flashing and started dumping coins into a slot at the bottom that looked like a clown's metal mouth. A loud "Bing!" split my ears each time it spit out a coin and it seemed to go on forever. I looked down the row and both the oldies were looking at me. They weren't happy, they weren't sad. When the Bing!-ing and the flashing and whirling lights stopped, the old lady's eyebrows flickered and she went back to her exercise routine. The old man gave me a little smile and turned away, too. I was sort of relieved I didn't have to high-five these guys.

For a three dollar spin, I'd won sixty bucks. Sixty! I couldn't believe it. I scooped the coins into my bucket and, figuring it would never let anyone win for another century or so, got up and resumed my quest to break the bank. I felt great. I almost ran over to another slot down the way and pumped in some coins, hit the button, waited, and as soon as the tumblers bounced to a halt, moved on just as fast. Hit and run. Hit and run. I'd only stop if the machine kicked out some coins, which happened a few times, then I'd pump them back in and either push the button or pull the lever. I was a proverbial Dirvish. But after I'd almost circled the floor, I was getting bored with the slots. I revised my plan. A few more slots, then I'd move closer to the centre and the table games. Same plan, though, play a few hands at each, changing all the time.

I looked around me. An aisle leading to the centre was about two rows of slots away. Eyeing it, I moved to the first machine in the first row, plunked in three coins are hit the button.

"Hey, what the fuck do you think you're doing! That's my fucking machine!"

The voice came from my right and was accompanied by a large woman dressed in living room curtains and plastic flip-flops. Her eyes were huge. The machine started that Bing!-ing blare. Lights flashed. Coins slapped down. The lady's eyes got bigger. She somehow managed to bring her eyebrows down to her nose and her upper lip over her nose holes. "You fucking thief! You fucking thief!" she screamed moving one step closer to me. "You stole my money. That's my machine! I've been playing these machines for six straight hours," she said pointing to four in a row starting with the one that wouldn't shut up with all the clanging and Binging and hurting my eyes with the flashing. "You watched me play, didn't you, you scum bag! You saw it was about to pay off, didn't you, you prick!"

"No. No. Really. I didn't know. I didn't know!" I said, literally assuming the pose of a beggar; hands out, bent over, head lowered. I looked over at the slot. The coins were still filling the metal mouth.

"Help! Help! Thief!" the woman screamed, looking around. For the cops? Shit, I didn't know. I must have done something completely wrong. I didn't know the rules. A whole posse of senior citizens had now surrounded us. I was screwed. I was going to be massacred by the boney fingers and uncut yellowing nails of a dozen maniacal nursing home escapees.

"No! Listen. No need for that," I said, still in the beggar mode. "Listen to me, I didn't know . . . ."

"What's the problem here?" This voice, from behind me, sounded official.

"This bastard muscled in on my machine just as I was about to play it. Shoved me aside. Practically threw me to the fucking ground, he did. And it paid off. That should be MINE!"

"That true?" I tuned around. The voice belonged to a large man with a badge hanging from the jacket pocket. Security. He looked a bit like a CSIS guy but his eyes were bored, not angry.

"No, really, I didn't know she was playing it! Honestly. She can *have* the money. I don't care . . ."

"Was it your money in the slot?"

"Yes! But I didn't push her aside. I didn't even see her until I hit the button. Look if I broke some rule, I'm really sorry but . . ."

The Security guy looked over my shoulder. "Molly, be honest with me."

"It should be my money!" she said, stepping back a bit.

"Molly?"

"It's not fair!" she said.

"It's not fair, it's not fair," others in the crowd chanted.

The Security guy reached out and, after asking with his eyes, took my bucket, went to the slot, scooped the coins into it and handed it back to me. His eyes told me to take it and move on to another area. As I walked away, I heard him say, "Molly, I've warned you before and I'm going to warn you again. Behave." And then I heard the "Boos!" It could have been a Maple Leafs game.

I went, head slightly down like a perp running the photographers' gauntlet, straight to the centre and the table games area. Thankful I had reached some inner sanctum where the clients were at lest thirty years younger and civilized.

I was catching my breath and feeling better when I spied a really pretty girl standing near a roulette table. She had this frightening grimace on her face. And a guy, a really handsome guy, was standing beside her and he was saying, "Gimme the cheque, babe. I'm real close. I can feel it.

I'm going to hit big, I know it," and she was just looking at him and saying nothing. I thought she might cry, she was misting up, but terror was also in those crystal eyes.

"Give me the fucking cheque," he hissed. "Christ, it's *my* cheque, for fuck's sake!"

She reached into her purse and handed it to him, as if she were handing him a used Kleenex, and he ran off toward the wickets. When he left, I maneuvered around to the other side, near the Pit Boss, and waited.

The man was back in two minutes tops, with cash in his hand. He went straight to the table, passed it over to the croupier. In a loud voice, the croupier called out over his shoulder, "two hundred" and handed the guy his chips. He put them all on one number. The wheel spun, the ball dropped. The guy looked like he'd been shot. The girl had already turned her back, was walking out, and I couldn't see her face. I was glad I couldn't. And in that instant I knew I didn't want to be in this place. I'd never been in a Casino before, of course, but I'd never had a lottery ticket in my life, either, and knew now I hadn't missed a thing.

After I cashed out my bucket, I called Abdul from a pay phone on the wall, then tried to find my way out of the place to the front doors. It isn't all that easy for some reason. I wandered in circles, jiggling some change in my pocket. I wanted to get out of there so fast that I didn't even know how much I had won on the slot. I decided I had had a genuine *Moment*. It would be known as a *Geriatric Hell Moment*.

At this point I should tell you that my parents didn't like gambling, which is probably why I wanted to go to a Casino. They didn't even like lottery tickets. They thought they were for suckers. "Legalized taxation of the poor," my mother said. "Illegitimate false hope," my father said. The odds alone, they said, were enough to make it transparent, they both said. I knew it was the hope thing, though. They saw hope as a weakness. "You don't hope for something, you go out and get it," my father said.

Now, my parents weren't neanderthals about this. This applied to adults, not kids. When I was growing up, they let me hope Santa Claus would come for Christmas and bring me a bicycle, and they never stopped me from hoping the Tooth Fairy would drop a fiver under my pillow for the first incisor, a ten spot for the next one, only now I knew I should have hoped for a gold wafer for that third one. And, of course, I hoped the Easter Bunny would drop a few hundred chocolate eggs in my basket, which he always did. No, it was only when I got older my parents popped the hope bubble with their speeches about the weak and illogical in society. Being a kid, I ignored what they were saying. It was like the dentist telling you to floss. You always say, "yeah, sure," because if you say "no," or "piss off," the bastard will give you a lecture that will bring tears to your eyes with boredom. But eventually I did get it, but it was my doing, not my parents.

When I was fourteen, I hoped, really hoped, Julie Sumner would give me a blow job, just like she did every other guy in my class. They said she had cheeks like a chipmunk and could get both nuts in her mouth at the same time. God, I hoped and hoped and hoped she would blow me, too, but she never did. I'd hang around her locker, chatting with her like she was just another girl in the class, and she never even gave me a hint that she'd drop to her knees and do me right then and there. Never. That's what made me think of what my father said; that you don't hope to get anywhere, you go out and ask for it, and even if you don't get what you ask for, at least you know where you stand and can get on with life instead of moping around thinking what might have been. I took his advice. I went right up and asked Julie for a blow job. She wound up and, with what could only be called a first-class upper cut, flattened me with one punch, leaving me on the linoleum outside the gym doors with the words: "And I thought you were the only decent boy in this whole goddamned school!" And she left. And she never came back to school again. No one knew why, and I couldn't tell.

I have often thought about what became of her but each time I do I get the crazy guilts, which makes your back sweat. Not a nice feeling. I imagine her leaving school and becoming a hooker, but that would be a stereotype, wouldn't it? She could just as easily become a world-famous brain surgeon, although she would have changed her name so no one would know what an artist she was when she was younger. I'd ask you to drop me a line if you knew what happened to her but there's a growing chance that it would be a bit futile under the circumstances.

I thought maybe Abdul would have skipped town, but when I finally found the front door, there he was, smiling like I'd handed him a dowry and asked for his daughter's hand. "Let's go look at The Falls close up," I said.

CHAPTER NINE

Abdul didn't seem to be all that enthusiastic about The Falls, as we crossed the street on foot from the parking lot and made our way down to the edge of the water. I was. It was amazing. Okay, I know, I'm not the first one to say it, but really . . . .

You can stand there and look right where The Falls flows straight down over the cliff. It's green, and shallow, and fast, and it draws you in. I swear, it hypnotizes you. You can almost feel yourself falling over the railing and getting swept away. It's a wonder more people don't jump. It would be so easy to do.

Abdul wasn't beside me when I turned around to talk to him about it. He was standing back about ten feet, his middle eastern face was drained of its muddy color, his mouth slack.

"Abdul, look at this!" I yelled. You have to be loud. Everyone says the water roars. I don't think so. I think it's more like a loud purr. Roaring is meant to scare the shit out of you but purring is what makes you instantly recognize a benevolent calmness cloaking ferocity. It'll bite if you cross it. But most of the time it just reminds you it can and will if you force the issue. As for Abdul, he just shook his head when I yelled back at him.

"Come on, what's the matter. You've seen this?" Once again, he shook his head. It was jerky. "What's the matter?" I asked, walking back to him, ready to take his arm.

"No no no," was all he said.

"What's the matter?"

"I am not going near there," he said, pointing at the edge.

"Why not?"

"Water is death," he said. I looked around to see whether that death guy with the scythe was standing there or something. Nobody. Just a bunch of Japanese tourists taking pictures of each other leaning over the railing and making faces like they were about to fall in.

"What do you mean?" I tugged at his sleeve but he wasn't budging. In fact, he was pulling away harder. So I went along with it. "Let's go over there and have a coffee," I said.

A place with chairs and tables was outside a restaurant a hundred feet back from The Falls. Abdul went without any trouble, sat down where I placed him and I got a couple of coffees. He was gripping the table when I got back.

"What gives, Abdul? What do you mean water is 'death?' You made it sound like, well, water would kill you?"

"It does," he said.

"You've got to be kidding," I said. "We need water, if we *don't* have water we'll die."

"That is right," he said.

"So?"

"If you do not have water, you will die. But if you do have water, you might also die." He took a sip of the coffee and made a face.

"No good?"

"This is not coffee, it is flavored water." I took a sip. Tasted like coffee to me.

"You're not making sense," I said.

Abdul looked at me for what seemed like a long time, as if he were studying me, seeing whether I could be trusted with a secret. I guess I could because he started explaining. "You see, my people come from a very small village . . ."

"You said you were Canadian, born in Toronto?"

"Yes, but my parents, their parents and generations before them, all came from this little village and they did not have water. Or, sometimes they did, but not much, it depended upon the winter before, but at many other times they had none."

"What did they do, truck it in?"

He looked at me as if I were a small child. "No," he said, "they would go down to the next village where they had water."

"And they would give your relatives some . . ."

"No, not always."

"They'd buy some?"

"No, if those villagers did not have enough to give, they did not have enough to sell."

"So what'd your family do?"

"They would go to war for the water. My family would kill them. That is why water is death."

"You're shitting me!"

"No, I am telling you the truth."

"They always won, then. Of course they did, otherwise you wouldn't be here, right? How'd they manage that?"

"They fought harder."

"Jeezes. Didn't the other villagers ever win?"

"No, never."

"So your family were better warriors."

"No. Because they had nothing to lose, they always won."

"But they never knew that when they went into battle, right?"

"That did not matter."

"Didn't matter? You're supposed to know you're going to win *before* you go to war, or you'd be stupid to go to war, right? I mean, who goes to war thinking they might lose and die?"

"Everybody, if they are honest. But dying is not the problem. If you do not have water, you are going to die. If you need water, you might die. Which is better?"

I thought about that a bit but, still, it all seemed a bit barbaric. "You've got to be a little afraid of dying, no?"

"No, of course not. We all die. As you people quaintly say, you start dying the second you are born. It is just a matter of when and how."

Abdul was getting more interesting all the time. "I can't get my mind around how casually you take all this dying business. For instance, you say water is death, but you were born here so how could you believe all that?"

"It is history. Only the selfish ignore history because its lessons stand in the way of an impatience to achieve false goals. Family history is stronger still, it is genetic, part facts of the past and inclinations to act in the future that are ingrained in your inner being. Family histories are passed down orally and in each retelling, the facts are unconsciously adjusted to the present to sustain the underlying lessons learned in the past. They exist to protect you. They are almost always fatal if ignored. I did not fight for water and kill to win it. But my family did. The lesson is waters' power to motivate one to kill another. It is life. It is death. One cannot have one without the other."

"But, I mean, you can't actually believe it applies now, do you?"

"If you poison all the water in the United States of America, what would the Americans do to have the vast Canadian water resources that exist right next door to them? Would not the villagers there come to the villages here? Remember the lessons of my family: The difference between asking and demanding is believing the consequences are irrelevant."

"Dying is irrelevant."

"There is nothing ignoble about dying. You all end up in the same place."

"You mean heaven?"

"If that is what you call it."

"How do you know it's real? How do you know it's not just some trick to keep you fighting?"

"It would not matter. You never stop fighting for water. You simply accept it could kill you. But then, you know how you are going to die. It is how you die that matters in this life."

"Painfully."

"You do not know that. You might just get shot and fall asleep, but then you would wake up in Paradise, so it does not matter. You will end up in Paradise no matter what. It is only a matter of when."

"You're not afraid of dying?"

"Oh no. I do not want to die like a dog; I think that might cause me to lose a few opportunities in Paradise, but I am not afraid of dying."

I sipped my coffee and looked back out at the tourists and the mist billowing up from the Falls. I thought about Abdul's words but, for instance, I'd never seen a dog die a bad death. I'd heard about dogs being too old and being put to sleep, but around here, they all seemed to live a pretty good life. Not that I had first-hand knowledge about that. My parents wouldn't have a dog. Apparently dogs were allergic to the leather in Bentleys and Jaguars and you couldn't have them in those cars, or any other cars they had, so we couldn't have dogs. Or cats. Or any pets, for that matter. You had to make sacrifices for some things, according to my parents. Oh, I'd heard Abdul loud and clear but I knew I'd have to digest what he said to grasp its weightiness. And as I sat there, I put together the digesting bit with forbidden stuff and remembered another thing my parents wouldn't let me have: Candy. Sweet stuff. Put everything together and I had this urge to share with Abdul, unlike the Iranian villagers who didn't want to share and ended up being killed.

"Okay, that's fascinating and all, but let's get the hell outta here," I said. Abdul was on his feet before I could put my paper cup down on the table. "Let's go to Niagara-on-the-Lake."

My parents took me to the Shaw Festival in NotL once and we saw this play. It bored the shit out of me. But then we walked around the town and every few feet, or so it seemed to me, were these fudge shops and kids were in there blowing their brains out in them. Not me, though. My parents just shook their heads. It wasn't a brothel or a strip club but it seemed illicit and I wanted some. "How about it? Abdul, we could go and get some fudge."

"Fudge?"

"Yeah. You know what it is, right?"

"Of course, I do."

"Really, what's it like?"

"You've never had fudge?"

"No." I was going to explain but threw that thought away.

"It's very sweet. Pure sugar, really."

"Great, let's get on it.

"I agree. I could bring some back to my children," Abdul said.

The drive to Niagara-on-the-Lake winds down beside the Niagara River from The Falls and it's where the river empties into Lake Ontario. The town itself is on a small point and used to be where the first government of Ontario set itself up. It wasn't called that. It was called Upper Canada, and Niagara-on-the-Lake itself was called Newark but what the hell. It's historic with a fort and everything. The fort was way better than the play I saw. Anyway, the drive is very pleasant for geriatrics but not very exciting for me so I got to thinking on the way again about things other than trees and old houses.

"Abdul, how do you know there's a Paradise?"

"Because I do."

"But how do you *really* know?"

Abdul was silent for a while. Then his head shot up a bit and he looked at me through the mirror. "You are a Christian, right?" I nodded. "Well, did not your Profit say that if it was not true, he would have told you?"

"Prophet?"

"You call him Jesus."

"I think he was supposed to be called the Son of God."

"Prophet. Jesus, Son of God. Same thing, no? And he told the people who followed him how to live and he did it because God told him to, correct? And then he said that if you believed him, you would go to Paradise?" He was spying me in the mirror again.

"Ah, I guess," I said, "but I think you go to Heaven and live in a room in a big mansion or something."

To tell you the truth, I was confirmed by no less than the Bishop of Toronto and sort of believed in everything the teaching reverends told me, but when I started going to the big church on sundays, the Canon stopped teaching about miracles, wine and bread parties, and then basically just begged for money every week. This was confusing because one of the lessons I was taught in the work-up to the bishop throwing water at me was the one about the camel: ". . . it is easier for a camel to go through the eye of a needle than for a rich man to enter into the Kingdom of God." And yet, it was okay for the church to beg for money. Or confiscate it from the rich people every week. When I started thinking about it, it got worse. If you took the lesson literally, it condemned every rich guy. Back two thousand years ago, maybe all the rich guys were evil, but what about my father? He was rich. And everyone said he was a good guy. Everyone. He was a surefire candidate to get in. And so were a lot of the fathers and mothers who went to our church. So I stopped going.

And you know when you stop practicing something, you tend to get a little rusty? I was rusty and just winging it.

"Mansions, tents, camels, Paradise, Heaven, it is probably all the same." Abdul said.

"But that's a bit hard to take, when you get right down to it. I mean, millions of people die every day and it'd have to be a pretty big mansion to get us all in there."

"Why could it not be that big?"

"Well, I mean, really, take a look at the earth. We'd have run out of room thousands of years ago, wouldn't we?"

"But what if earth is actually small?" Abdul said. "What if it is like a grain of sand on a big beach and we are very very small people. How do you know that is not true? And you are a Christian, and you think that when you die your body stays here and your spirit goes to Heaven. How big can a spirit be?"

"You don't believe in spirits?"

"I prefer to think I go to Paradise looking just like this," he said, giving me a big smile of those mahogany teeth.

"That matters?"

"How are you going to have sex if you do not have a body?" he said.

That was a jolt. I'd *never* made it with anyone. And then another jolt. If I were still a virgin when I croaked, and Abdul was right about all this and there really was a Heaven or Paradise or whatever, they might put me in one of those big mansion rooms where I wouldn't need sex because I'd never had it on earth and they might figure I wouldn't miss something I'd never had. And when I thought about *that*, it made me sweat. I'd have to get laid. If nothing else, that *had* to a priority. But I'd have to do a shit load of other stuff, too, so I'd be ready if both Pho and Abdul were right. So I *had* to try fudge and any other candy I could get my hands on, and all types of liquor – beer, wine, and the hard stuff. The very best, mind you. My parents told me to always eat and drink the best at first so you can judge everything else like it later. It was good advice. For instance, Imperial Golden Osetra caviar from Iran ruined it for any other fish eggs, even Beluga.

But getting back to it, I didn't want to be fooled if there were really a Heaven and it had rules about these things. It had to have rules, right? Rules made sense because why would a two or three-year-old need fudge, booze or sex when they died? They couldn't really hang around with me or Abdul up there, could they? So there had to be rules about that kind of thing. Maybe there was something to all of this Heaven stuff, and maybe we all sort of know about it but it's not, like, right out there in front of our faces. Maybe that's why nobody's ever come back and said, "yup, it's true, it's there, and they have unlimited Rusty Nails and you don't puke." I know, Jesus is supposed to have told us that. But he was just *one* guy, and he was, like, two thousand years ago.

You know, I might believe some guy, or girl, who had nothing to do with religion if one or the other came back to say it's true, and then set up a travel agency for unbelievers so they could go *and* come back. Call it *Out of This World Vacations* and it'd be the first true company title in history. That would be a sure fire way to spread the word. Nothing better than word-of-mouth endorsement. But then I thought about a possible flaw; if we actually *knew* there was a Heaven or Paradise or whatever, I suppose it's all we would think about and then we'd never be afraid so when the hordes came down from the village above for our water we'd just roll over and die because we'd get eternal fudge, booze and sex. And then the bloody problem of population control came to mind and how that might be cured by all this but I put it out of my mind just about as fast as it came in; when I was in a position to contribute to that problem, I would be on firmer ground to think about it.

Abdul found a spot right out front of one of the fudge shops on the north side of the main street, which was lucky because it was about to close, as was the whole town. We went in and got pounds of the stuff; chocolate, maple, fudge fudge, some white goop that tasted more like pure sugar than anything else, and hauled it back to the cab and ate a little of each until I thought my teeth would crack. Abdul was moaning. I know it sounds crazy but it was about dinner time and I was already hungry. The Casino steak and fudge notwithstanding, the thought of a good dinner with Abdul was comforting, not to mention the thought of trying out my good booze and wine theory.

My parents always said that while Niagara-on-the-Lake was quaint, it was not a dining destination, with the exception of the Peller Estates dining room just outside of town and a place called *On The Twenty*, which was attached to another winery but was way farther out of town. Peller made wine, too. They knew the guy who built the winery for the Peller family, a guy with way too much hair, smiled all the time and was generally thought of as a good guy. Peller was a good guy, too, but they knew the builder, not Peller. I'd seen the winery sign as we were driving in from The Falls so I steered Abdul where that was and, sure enough, we found it. Not hard to do, actually; it was huge modern house-like building in the middle of a million rows of vines.

When we walked in, Abdul started to get fidgety and turned around. "I should wait outside," he said. "I should not be here."

I reached his arm and stopped him. "You're my guest. You stay. Actually, I insist. You want the rest of your money, right?"

"They may ask me to leave."

"Why would they do that? I won't let them. Besides, look at the place. It's almost empty."

"They have a way of saying an empty place is actually full, you know."

"Why would they do that?"

"It is just the way."

"Don't talk crazy. I've never heard that before."

"That is because . . ." and he trailed off. This really strikingly good looking woman with a slit up her dress came waltzing out to the front door and smiled. God, her smile could have melted ice cream. And she had these teeth that were perfect, not horsey big, not kid little, adult teeth, teeth you would want really really close to your own teeth, and given my thoughts of fudge and booze and beer and wine and sex, I thought this was all going to come together as a *Bazoom Moment!*

"Do you have a reservation?" she asked in a voice that flowed out of her mouth, through my head, straight down my spine and around through my waist to the front.

"Well, no, I was just passing through the area with my friend and I remembered a friend telling me about this place, that I had to come if I were in the neighborhood, and so here we are and . . ."

"Well, that's fine," she said, "will it be just for two?"

"Yes, yes," I said. I was in love. Seriously.

She led us to a table by a window overlooking the vineyard. It was still light outside and we could see along the rows stretching and bowing to the horizon. Actually, it was probably a little early for dinner; we never ate at home before 7.30 at night, usually eight, so I figured that was why the place was almost empty. A little old lady and man, probably in their hundreds, were eating four tables away, leaning way over their plates, their hunchbacks growing from the backs of their chairs.

Another woman came by with a pitcher of water and poured some into our glasses. "Could I have a scotch rocks to start? And you Abdul?"

The woman looked at me sadly. "Sir, I'm afraid this is a winery and we only have wine." And then Abdul piped up: "I do not drink alcohol."

"Of course, of course, and you're driving, after all," I said.

"But perhaps a glass of Ice Cuvée to start while you look at the menu?" she asked.

"Yes, that would be perfect." I didn't have a clue what she was talking about. My mind was numb from my idiocy. If I was going to do the booze and beer experiment, it would have to be later, obviously. Maybe this was some ethereal plan to make me pace myself. A good plan, as it turned out, because with each course, they would bring a different wine, and by the end I would be squiffed and happy. But Abdul looked uncomfortable sitting with his back to the window watching the staff walk around.

"Abdul, let's change places, okay?" His eyes went up, like he didn't understand. I stood up and – I'll bet it was his instinct – he got up, too, and we changed seats. When he sat down, with his back to the restaurant, seeing only out the window, he seemed a little more at ease.

"So you believe that when you go to Paradise, you go looking just like you are and you get to have all the good stuff you've had on earth, right?"

"Something like that," Abdul said.

"But you're a Muslim and you don't drink?"

"That is true."

"So when you go to Paradise, you won't be in any bar."

"Also true."

"Then the red necks win, don't they? I mean, they'll have the bars to themselves up there. You'll be excluded, just like they want."

"No, because we exclude ourselves."

I thought about that. He was right. Of course he was, he'd thought about this a lot more than I.

To start I had the "white bean, pig and truffle soup," because if a chef in a place like that names his soup *pig soupe*, he's got a sense of humor. And a gift. My God it was good. It had this big hammy flavor and came with a wine called a *Gamay Noir*. I expected something really red and strong despite the bad spelling because I'd had venison and boar and they were all distinctly stronger than beef or pork. My father called the taste "gamey." That's why I thought the wine would be strong, too. But the wine was nearly pink and instead of gamey, it left me with the taste of bananas and some other kind of fruit in my mouth. It just did. I liked it. I instantly understood why winos sprawled out in the parks in downtown Toronto drank this stuff. It wasn't sweet like grape juice but it was still fruity. And it didn't make your eyes water like a Rusty Nail did. If I had a choice of what beverage I would drink to lie around the park every day, I'd choose wine over booze. I told this to Abdul, who was drinking water. I'm not entirely sure but I think he rolled his eyes.

By the time I'd finished the glass, I was starving for the main course, even after this big soup, the wine, the fudge, the steak . . . I'd ordered duck, except it didn't taste like any duck I'd had in Chinatown or in a French restaurant, it tasted more like rare steak, and it came with a wine called *Cabernet* made by Franc. He was probably the winemaker, and probably from Germany given how he spelled his name. And this wine, unlike the *Gamay Noir,* had a kick to it and sort of made my mouth dry up a little. The funny thing was, it tasted like that on its own but when I sipped it with a mouthful of duck, it had a different taste, sort of smoother and less puckery. For dessert I had a chocolate gingerbread thingy and this time Franc sweetened up the *Cabernet*.

Abdul seemed to have hit the jackpot, too, although he looked at everything like it was a sin or something. He had this slab of melting fat over a salad to start, little round lamb steaks cooked rare and topped with some clear sauce for the main course, and a butter tart, except it wasn't really a butter tart but he said it was almost as sweet and he liked it. He liked it all, he said, but he also looked like he had stolen something. I didn't show him the bill, either. He would have really thought it was a sin then.

I was so wrapped up in the food and wine that I had all but ignored Abdul during the meal. Rude. At the end I was sipping a really sweet wine I figured they made after the harvest when they made the real wine, and although it was sweet it didn't crack your teeth like the Wild Duck crap my friends drink. The winemaker, maybe it was Franc, must have found a way of dissolving sugar in ice cold wine without leaving that rubber ring on the bottom like my mother did making Jell-O. Anyway, as I was sipping this, I got back to old Abdul sitting there.

"About this Paradise thing, the guy who talked about it, Jesus, you called him a Prophet, right? Well, I think he'd have more cred if he came back like he said he would and told us again. Don't you think?"

"Cred?"

"Credibility. Street credibility."

"Maybe he has come back," Abdul said.

"I think that would make the nightly news, don't you?"

"Not if he came back before Television was invented. Or radios."

What *was* Abdul thinking? "No, no, you see, that's the problem. I think more people would be convinced there was a Heaven or Paradise if someone my age came back and said he'd seen it."

"How do you know he has not?"

"Like I said . . . "

"Let me put it this way," Abdul said. "Jesus was a Prophet, correct?"

"Son of God, I believe."

"As you said. A prophet is someone who says things will happen and they do. So people call him a prophet, and they believe him, correct?"

"I guess so."

"So let us settle on that. Jesus was a Prophet and he lived more than two thousand years ago. He said he would return, did he not? Now you say he has not. But a man, very much like your Jesus, we call him a Prophet, too, the Prophet Mohamed, was born almost 600 years after Jesus. He preached just about the same things as Jesus. And it you study other religions, even Asian ones but some modern ones, too, like the Mormons, they have their Prophets, or people who say about the same things, and say they were told by God to say them."

"They *all* can't be the same guy . . ."

"Why not? If they are here just to make us better people, better thinkers, why not? I have told you, I have children and I want them all to grow up to be good people. But, you know, they all think differently. Some listen to reason – not many at that age – some do things because I threaten them. Yes, I do, and I'm not ashamed of it. For instance I have spanked them. My third son, we lived on a busy street, he ran out on the road even though I was yelling at him to stop. I ran after him, caught him, dragged him to the side of the road and spanked him hard and told him to never, ever run out on a street again. And he never did. His sister and brother, who watched this, never did, either, but I did not have to spank them to learn this lesson. They learned for their own reasons. My other son learned because he did not want me to hurt his bottom. My daughter? I think she learned because all she has ever wanted to do in this life is to please her daddy; she is the little light of my life, I tell you."

Abdul paused, looked up at the ceiling and smiled. "Praise Allah." Then looked back at me.

"So if you are God and want to teach all the people, and you know that some people will not listen or believe the God of their enemies, why not send down a Prophet in another disguise. Would God not see that nomad tribes of the sand would never follow a foreigner's God? What would be wrong if He sent down a Prophet designed specially for them so his message, virtually the same message as the ones rejected, be received and believed? Send down another Prophet, the Prophet Mohammed, or the philosopher Confucius or Joseph Smith."

"So you're saying Jesus has already returned a bunch of times?"

"In essence, that might be true."

"That's why you say Heaven and Paradise are the same."

"I do not know the truth because Allah's plan for us is unknown, it is not a science that relies on proof. I only know what I believe. And what I want to believe. I believe in Allah. Millions of Muslims such as me do and it makes us unified and strong. What makes us weak is what we individually *want* to believe. I want to believe Allah did not tell our Prophet to say we must kill nonbelievers. I do not want to believe the United States is Satan. I do not want to believe women are inferior or that they should remain hidden. But many others do, as you know from your nightly news. So I ask, 'are these things so?' but no one can answer correctly because there is no proof, just interpretations of Allah's word as relayed by our Prophet through the Q'oran. But others want to believe the opposite. It is this state of wanting to believe that is at the centre of the problem.

"There are as many interpretations of the word of Allah as there are interpreters. First the conflict was theological and healthy. Now it has been poisoned by killing, one faction overpowering the others to be recognized as Allah's true and faithful followers. They speak and then demonstrate their power. We want to believe that Allah said we should not kill anyone or beat our wives or end our own lives. We want to believe that He would not want us to charge and punish people with Sixth Century laws and justice. But the others think He does. You see, I want to believe they are wrong and evil and should be stopped. But I cannot prove they are, according to Allah. And if I believe I am right, I must act against Allah's wishes and kill them. But I cannot because I believe – not *want* to believe but really *believe* – that I should not kill. And I will not. So I, like everyone who thinks like me, stand by and watch the western governments kill them. They do the work we believe should be done but will not do ourselves."

"Jeezes. I've never heard it put that way," I said, and meant it. I wanted to know something simple and this is what I got.

"Do you think less of me?" Abdul asked.

What a question! Until that morning, I hadn't thought about it at all. Now I was being asked to judge a religion, a cab driver's moral and religious character and whether the western world leaders were murderers or saviors. All I wanted was to have some fun. But then it occurred to me that Abdul was treating me like an adult and he deserved an adult answer. The problem was, I didn't have one. And the wine made me more inclined to fall off my chair laughing than pass judgement.

"Shit no, Abdul, but I don't think you can rely on me for advice. I mean, until today, I'd never ridden in a Chevrolet before."

The dining room at Peller was almost full by the time we left and I didn't have a chance to talk up the woman at the front, which was really too bad, although what with all this Abdul talk and the wine I was somehow a little less horny than usual but somehow more comfortable trying to get her attention, what with me paying cash, and all. Beautiful women overlook flaws in a man if he has scads of money, right? Even an age difference? If not, what the hell is money good for? It must be for this because, let's face it, most guys are butt ugly, very few Brad Pitts and George Clooneys out there, so given the choice, beautiful women would probably take the cash over the fairly decent looking loser, which would be me except for the money, right? But I knew as I walked out the big doors, even with all that wine, I'd be able to conjure her up that night in bed. And probably the next morning, too, so it wasn't a complete loss.

Except for the fact that the Casino left me with a slightly sleazy feeling, it had been a great day, and Abdul had turned out to be a really good guy. When he dropped me off, I told him to wait. I came back and handed him two more wafers. I thought he was going to cry. I almost started crying too, for no damn good reason except how I was generally feeling these days. I didn't know whether Abdul was full of shit about this whole prophet and heaven stuff, but he deserved the tip.

CHAPTER TEN

The last time I saw the doctor, he told me that I should listen to my body, that my body would tell me what I should do on any given day, what I should eat, whether I should take it easy or go balls out. I didn't wake up the day after the Casino until about 11.30 in the morning and I felt a little slow, sluggish, as it were, not in any pain or anything, just sort of mellow and uninspired. So I listened to my body and thought it was telling me to hang around home and maybe do some laundry. And as soon as I thought about that, I knew the Doc was right; laundry seemed doable suddenly instead of a boring chore. I have heard of people who actually like doing laundry. I wonder if they are permanently sluggish people?

Now, you've got to know I'd never done laundry before. Not really. The only time I actively thought about it was when I shit my pants after the Jackson Pollack incident but as you might remember, I threw out the underwear instead. I have never met a washing machine or a dryer. I've seen them advertised on TV but that's about it. If I had to go out and buy them, I wouldn't have clue what to look for, what to put in them, what *not* to put in them, except maybe a cat or a small dog. I'm not a complete doofus. But I *did* know from newsgroup sites that Laundromats were great places to pick up women and, I suppose, learn how to use the machines.

This one, *alt.women.pickup.needy*, explained in detail what to look for in a Laundromat. Just like in real estate, the consensus on line was that it's location, location, location. I don't get why, but there it is. Anyway, only two sorts are worth considering. The first is the "Yummy Mummy" Laundromat. That's one where hot mothers do their wash. They're at the Laundromat because they're horny and their husbands don't look at them the same way anymore and they want a quickie without strings because they have kids, after all, and the last thing they want are more complications their lives. Spotting the "prey" in these Laundromats. Just by looking at these Mummies. you know they have washing machines at home.

The other type is the student Laundromat, typically near a university, because that's where horny co-eds do their laundry and, generally speaking, they all like to fuck and then fuck off. If they want a lasting relationship, they hang around the law school or hospitals and sometimes, if they're smarter than average, the engineering schools, but they have to be pretty slutty to hang around engineers, although, again, I don't know why this is. But if they just want to flirt and size up your jeans, they go to Laundromats. The ones who want a fast fuck fold their underwear in front of you and look into your eyes to see whether you're cool or crying, the latter being bad, the former good.

The Yummy Mummies on the link from the newsgroup all look hot and slutty as hell, especially soaped up when the washing machines explode. But they also gave me the creeps; I guess when you grow up with a mother like mine, with all your friends drooling when she walks in or out of a room, it gets way too creepy to think about it. I could imagine what it would feel like if their kids walked in on them. That would be bad, bad, bad. Co-eds, on the other hand, were built to breed and even if they didn't know that in so many words, they *felt* that and sometimes it overwhelmed them, so even a dork might get lucky in a fit of spin cycle madness. Sounded good to me.

Laundromats or the opera? No contest. But the article warned, it wasn't good enough just to show up. You had to become a "presence" in the Laundromat, because the competition was ramping up exponentially as word spread about this previously little-known treasure trove. The best trick involved reading. If you were near a technical college like Ryerson down on Church, pretending to be deep into a computer manual was a good thing. A general liberal arts university, like the University of Toronto a few blocks north and west of Ryerson, required reading philosophy or something completely off the wall like a cookbook to show how versatile and broad-minded you are. "Broad minded."Get it?

Also in play was what you were wearing. Despite the fact that it was a Laundromat and you were, in effect, proclaiming you were dirty in the first place, you had to look and dress cleanly. Yummy Mummies and co-eds alike insisted on cleanliness, even if they weren't thinking that way. And the kicker to all this, the consensus agreed, was that co-eds in particular were pigs in private. Their rooms and apartments were filthy. All of them. Only the never-get-fucked co-eds were neat freaks. All the fuckees were slobs. What they wanted was to come back to your place to ball and they didn't want to go back to a place as filthy as theirs, so you had to dress and appear as if you had a maid at least three times a week. Dishes were an exception. No one washed dishes, and dirty dishes in the sink meant you cooked, and if you cooked, you could cook for them in a pinch, since they didn't cook, or couldn't, and certainly would rather you took them to a restaurant or took them to your place, after which they would at the very least go down on you if the meal was decent, and if it was spectacular they might even say "you can do *anything* you want to me."

Anyway, all this wearing clean clothes and reading stuff was important, and looking helpless by asking how to work the machines was your introduction, which wouldn't be a stretch for me since I knew nothing about laundry. The ultimate was to look like a lost puppy, one who was clean and read something appropriate to the location. The magazine suggested looking in the mirror and trying to make a slightly sad, confused expression. This could be achieved by either thinking about a puppy or kitten, depending upon whether you were a cat or dog person, being crushed by a garbage truck. If you were so psychotic that *that* thought didn't do the trick, you could put one hand in your pocket and squeeze your nuts until you thought you'd cry. The latter was to be used only as a last resort because it might hinder performance later. All of this seemed to make great sense.

The clean clothes bit was going to be tricky. I didn't have a pair of clean underwear, which is why I thought about doing laundry in the first place. I went around the bedroom with a plastic garbage bag picking up underwear and sniffing each one, trying to find the least objectionable. I settled on a pair that I might have slept in and dribbled into only slightly. Then I went around and picked up all the shirts and pants and sweaters and socks, smelling the socks as I did, and stuffing them into the bag until it was full and way too heavy. This laundry bit wasn't supposed to be exercise, for Christ's sake. When I was finished, I couldn't believe how big my bedroom was. It was huge. And the floor! I'd forgotten it had this beautiful blond hardwood and a silk oriental rug. I shook my head before going to the bathroom where I collected the towels and spied the overflowing wastepaper basket by the toilet. I got another garbage bag and emptied that, and then went into the kitchen and put the kitchen garbage bag in the green one and closed it up. I was on a mission. It was going well.

My jeans had a spot on the front leg; peanut butter, I think. I washed it off with a wet paper towel as best as I could and then let it dry. Looked better. Not perfect, but better. A shirt, which didn't smell, with a sweater over top, my loafers, no socks, and I looked okay. But I couldn't take *The Joy of Cooking* because that would make me look like the amateur I was, and I didn't have another cookbook. So I took my Drinks book, the one where I learned how to make a Rusty Nail. It also had a list of good liquor to buy. It suddenly occurred to me that everything was coming together: I was going to a Laundromat, not just any Laundromat but one where I could pick up a girl, maybe get laid, I could learn about the best booze, and if all else failed, get some clean clothes. I had just invented a new definition for the word, multitasking.

The yellow pages listed Laundromats and with the Google maps, I found one near the University of Toronto, I was pretty pumped about this laundry washing business.

The place was on College Street just north of the main campus, and as soon as I got out of the cab, I saw it. Actually, you couldn't miss it. Two huge glass windows stretched across the street, rows of machines ran down each side with a long row of ugly tables intersecting the middle. Vending machines with soap and fabric softener and other stuff I didn't know what to do with were screwed to the wall at the end, and two rows of bare florescent lighting ran down the entire length of the ceiling. This was not the Fallsview Casino. It was a murky fish tank. If you wanted to actually screw in there, you'd both have to be masochistic voyeurs. The atmosphere aside, the place had its attractions, namely a dirty blond and a dirty brunette, both wearing ripped jeans and T-shirts with no bras and perky tits that swayed and bounced as they stuffed stuff into the huge round washing machines. The blond also took out wet clothes and jammed them into a tumble drier and her T-shirt got wet and I damn near fainted before I could even throw the garbage bag up on the table and take my clothes out. Once I did, however, my Internet lessons kicked in.

I looked down at my laundry, up at a machine, down at the laundry again, rubbed my chin, up at the machines, shuffled my feet, looked down at the laundry again, fished around in my pocket for coins, eyed the detergent dispenser at the end, counted out some change, rubbed my chin, and peeked at the blond . . . She was supposed to be looking at me with motherly curiosity. She was not. She was folding clothes and smirking. Smirking! And shaking her head. I felt myself flush a little. The brunette farther down wasn't even paying attention to the show. She was ignoring the whole thing.

One of the things the newsgroup gurus said was that if you put dark stuff like black socks in with the white stuff, it drives women crazy because, apparently, you're not supposed to mix colors with whites. So once I got some detergent and read the package six times to make sure the two girls would sense my complete incompetence, I stuffed everything I could into a machine without regard to the colors. I closed the door and peered at the coin slot to give them time to come over and mend my ways. Nothing. I dropped a coin into the machine, hit the start button, watched the thing splash to life and froze. Still nothing. A peak; both were shaking their lowered heads and smirking. It occurred to me that they had read the same articles on line and I was ruining my clothes for nothing. *Shit!* I pulled out the Drink book, sat down in one of the most uncomfortable chairs I had every been in, and flipped open the book.

Scotch. Single Malts. *Shit. Boring.* Except that pretty soon, the thought of whacking back something called a Glenlivet sounded pretty damned good. I fished a piece of paper out of my pocket and wrote that down. Next was Grey Goose vodka, then Bombay Sapphire gin, Crown Royal Canadian whiskey, Johnny Walker Blue, not Black like I had been drinking with Drambuie, Baccardi 1857 . . . My machine stopped. I put the book and the list down on the table and went over to the washing machine. When I opened the door and a blast of clean clothes moistened my face, I saw the blond, basket of folded laundry under one arm, looking down at my list. She paused. Looked at me. Smiled.

"To buy list," I said.

"Really?"

"Ah, yeah."

The blond motioned with her eyes at the brunette. They knew each other. She nodded down to my list. The brunette's eyes went up when she read it.

"When?" the blond asked.

"On my way home, I guess," I said.

"Really," the blond said.

"Really," I said.

"I don't believe you," she said. "This is expensive. If you had this kind of money, you'd have your own machines." She nodded at the washers and driers.

"New rental," I said. "Haven't got any yet."

"Where do you live?"

"Down the street, a block north."

"Still don't believe you," she said.

"Well, come with me, then."

The blond looked at the brunette. "If I do, will you drive me home?"

"Nope, don't have a car, but I'll get a cab for you."

"Can't afford a cab."

"I'll pay for one."

"She comes too," she said, nodding at the brunette, who looked at me with a challenge in her eyes.

When my laundry was dry, they helped me fold it and stuff it back into the garbage bag. The conversation throughout was more of an inquisition than a normal conversation and I had to be quick on my feet for most of it, cool and aloof outside while trying to hide a constantly rising and falling erection mixed with a feeling of impending throw-up.

The blond was Christy, the brunette Doris, and they were, indeed, U of T students in second year, Liberal Arts, on their daddy's dime, living in a dorm having both been rejected by sororities for being both poverty-stricken and sluts. They said that. Sluts. That was one of the times I felt sick to my stomach. Really, I don't think I have ever been that excited in my life.

I got the cab to stop at the only liquor store he knew that carried all the best stuff, the main one downtown by the waterfront, and by the time we were back uptown, had dropped off the girls' laundry at their dorm and zipped over to my place, the cab bill was almost $45. When I peeled off five tens, the girls started to get fidgety, too. They got really twitchy when they saw my place, the oriental carpet, the farting chair, the sleigh bed. They looked at each other in silence. I knew I was in. I just *knew it*!

I lined up all the bottles on the living room table, got out some glasses, sat down with this stupid grin on my face, asked them to join me on the sofa, poured a shot of Glenlivet into three glasses, handed one to each girl, raised mine, said the immortal words, "bottoms up!" I sipped, and just then remembered I didn't have a condom.

And it happened again, only this time the *Speed Stick* tasted a bit like mud. I'd eaten mud once. Mud was wet. This was different. This was dry mud, and it burned. "Good," I said to the girls. "Mmmmmm," the blond said. "I'll say!" the brunette said. I waved at them and went to the kitchen, grabbed the plastic milk container, put the bagged milk carefully upright in the sink so it wouldn't spill out, filled the container with cold water and brought it back.

"We should probably sip water between drinks," I said, "to keep the tastes from ruining each other. So, whad'ya want to try now?"

If the Glenlivet was mud, then I imagined the Crown Royal was bog water, not that I have ever had bog water, but you get the idea. Gin, vodka, rum . . . by the time we got to the Tequila, I was having no trouble swishing the stuff down. Didn't even burn my throat anymore. So we started back at the Glenlivet and now I could taste it much better. I figure that's why all these things are called "acquired tastes." But it pays to acquire the taste in some ways because this good stuff was making us all laugh. And talk. The girls started talking like they knew me, or at least like they had seen me on campus and had sized me up and now that we were together, it was okay to talk like we knew each other. Does that make sense? It did to me, at the time.

"So what do you do?" Doris asked.

"Me?" I said, pointing at myself, as if there were someone else in the room. How clever is that?

"Sure, like, do you go to the university?"

"Ah, no actually I . . ."

"Where do you go to school then?" the blond asked.

"I don't," I said. "I sort of dropped out."

"So you work," said Doris.

"Yeah, I'm sort of a writer."

"A writer? You're kidding! What do you write about? Have I ever read anything you've written?"

"Probably not," I said. "It's all technical stuff." I was fighting with my head now. What the hell was I going to say? I didn't want to blow it. I'd had a boner from the second we got into the cab. I could barely push the cart in the liquor store without it sticking through my pants and wedging itself between the little metal bars. In the apartment, I had to adjust myself in a way that they wouldn't notice because if they noticed, they would have thought I was a perv for sure and they would have run from the place, and that was the last thing I wanted. What I wanted, well, I couldn't very well tell them, could I?

"Software, right?" Doris asked.

"Yes, exactly," I said. I wanted to look down to see if my boner was showing but I couldn't.

Doris thought we should probably have some food. Neither wanted pizza. Doris suggested chicken, so we went with that and she got on her cell phone and called Swiss Chalet for delivery and then talked to someone, and then I'm sure I saw her text someone else before joining us and rolling on the floor laughing about something. I can't remember what it was. It was hilarious, though.

The chicken came and just as we were popping fries into each other's mouths, the doorbell rang and five guys and two other girls arrived and Doris said they were her friends who were in the neighborhood and she didn't think I'd mind because if we drank all this booze ourselves we would probably die. And she was right about that, I suppose, because at this point I could stand but had a clear understanding why people shouldn't drive. As more people arrived, I remember asking Christy if she had a condom.

"Oh, sure," she said, "everyone always has them so don't worry about passing them out at your own party. You've done enough already."

I remember her saying that. I remember thinking, as well, that the reason I asked the question was not philosophical or sociological or even because I was a polite host, but it might as well have been any of those because it was definitely rhetorical at that point.

Want to know how I felt the next morning? Well, it's difficult to adequately describe in words but try this. The next time you tear the last square of toilet paper from the roll, just for fun, rip the cardboard tube into pieces and stuff them into your mouth. All of them. Don't be a chicken. Here's what happens. All the moisture in your mouth dries up. Bone dry. From your tongue, cheeks, everywhere, even under your tongue. It's hard to breathe. Eventually, as you desperately work it around to get some relief, a little piece of the cardboard gets lodged in your throat. You gag, a small one at first and then it becomes violent because the damn thing won't budge. Your head snaps forward with each gag. Your stomach clenches up every time your heart beats until you don't think you can stand it anymore. You try to pull the cardboard pieces out with your fingers but you can't do it in time. The heaves are on their own now. You need to tip your head back and hork as big a hork as you can to dislodge the cardboard from your throat. The pieces blast out but just as you think it's over, the muscles above your stomach feel punched and a stream of everything in your stomach spews out. And again. And again. Even when there's nothing more in your stomach.

Now imagine it's twice as bad. This is not, I repeat not, bubble gut. This is a series of out-of-control simultaneous light speed protons crashing in your body and turning the vital organs gelatinous and spewable.

The only other thing I could say about the next day was that it was still light when I woke up. But not for long. By the time I'd lived through the cardboard toilet paper torture, the sun was going down. That's depressing. It's one thing for someone to sleep all day, even on a weekend, and I used to do that all the time, although I don't know why because I have never, ever been drunk like that before, but it's an entirely different thing when you're supposed to be able to count the number of days you've got left and then waste one of them. And then you look around and see that it's going to take at least another day to clean up the house. Maybe more. *So* depressing.

In lipstick, on the bathroom mirror, were the words: "Thanks for the fun. Sorry you were too sick. I'll call. Chrissy." Underneath, in another handwriting, was a scrawl: "Yeah, right, and pigs fly."

This was hardly uplifting. First of all, what the hell did she mean by "too sick?" Too sick for what? Was she actually going to *do* me and I was too sick? If so, all that proton crashing didn't produce the Big Bang. That, too, was depressing. And then her signature: Chrissy. I'd been calling her Christy, with a "t", all day, all night. Jeezes. And who was the asshole who had access to her lipstick so he could write that flying pig crack? It wasn't going to be a good 24 hours.

I won't bore you with the clean up except to say the place was trashed. I checked the box springs and at least the bastards didn't find the gold wafers but the bed was a mess and I don't think I was responsible for it. Stain and spray marks peppered the oriental and the floor; the floor could be wiped clean, the oriental carpet could be blotted up because there's something in the fibers that naturally repel wet stuff, Shashi the carpet guy said, except cat piss. Then there were the bottles. Not only were mine there to clean up but someone must have brought the case of beer and I didn't notice. God, what a mess. The rum bottle had the most left, about three or four ounces, and when I popped the top and smelled to see if it was still rum and not someone's piss, it was all rum but I had to run to the can again and heave some dry ones for about five minutes. I don't think I'll ever drink rum again. Just to see, I smelled the others: Scotch, vodka, gin, even tequila and ouzo. They were just fine with me apparently. I'd smelled all these years before from my parents liquor cabinet, of course, so I could recognize them now. Crown Royal, for instance, smells pleasant, like a mild medicine, so I drank a little with room-temperature water and felt a little better for about half an hour. Then that same feeling came back, walking around carrying two bags of peat moss around my neck. I couldn't take any more. I had another Crown Royal and went back to bed.

Chapter Eleven

Maybe at this point I should explain a few things about this so-called "little diary," not that it's escaped your notice.

First, I'm not a writer, okay? I'm 18, after all. But Dr. Pho said I should consider making notes of what was going on after I left his office. He said it would probably be "useful," and for whatever reason, I got a notebook and began right after my father came home with the opera tickets. I didn't actually write too many sentences, just jotted down things in a sort of pigeon shorthand, things that stood out. But I purposefully left stuff out, too, because they were too mundane, like shopping for certain things, or because they'd probably turn you off. For instance, when I write that I get "weak" sometimes, I could go into all the gory details but it's irrelevant because while it happened sometimes, it didn't happen all the time and it got better. For instance, for no reason I can think of, I'd suddenly get a massive nose bleed. I know, I know, that's where all this started with my mother going batshit because I had a bloody nose sometimes. But now I mean blood everywhere. A virtual tap turned on in my nose. Both nostrils, too. I could understand it if I'd been picking my nose but since it triggered all that doctor stuff, I'd stopped being a nose picker.

I learned that three things were invaluable: Kleenex, toilet paper and those white kitchen trash bags into which you could throw the Kleenex you stuffed up your nose to stop the bleeding, or at least soak it up until it stopped by itself. Because *Nose Gushes*, as I came to call them, were always at the back of my mind and tempered my actions to a degree, I started to go into detail about the euphoria I felt when I stumbled onto a sale of Kleenex and toilet paper during one of the discount days at the drug store, but cut it out because, well, who the hell cares except me?

And it wasn't only Nose Gushes. Whenever I got one, blood would sometimes start seeping from my ears, too. Now, that freaked me out. It's like watching your brains pour out of your head. A nose bleed is a nose bleed. You get one whenever someone punches you in the face or you get whacked by a hockey stick and it's no big deal, but bleeding from the ears is downright freaky. So when I say in this diary "I got weak," it usually means *The Bleeds,* as the collective came to be known. Luckily, it usually happened at home and the one good thing about living alone is you don't have to wear clothes. Fresh blood washes off skin easily in the shower, dried blood not so much. So there I'd be with Kleenex stuck up my nose and Kleenex sprouting out my ears, no clothes, wandering around the house occasionally looking at myself in the mirror at this weird sight. Oh, and by the way, did I mention down below, too? Yup, after awhile, I'd start to bleed from my asshole. Kleenex up, down and all around the town at once. I'd look in the mirror and wonder if the Kleenex people could use me for an endorsement. I'd do it, you know.

At first I'd be sitting on the can, bleeding from every orifice, giving new meaning to the term, "bowl of red," and, I admit, feeling sorry for myself. Really, really sorry. I mean, what the hell did I do to deserve this? It's not as if I'd screwed a monkey, or killed a puppy, or hanged a cat on Hallowe'en, I'd been a pretty good kid, I think. No truancy, no jail time, no hanging with the wrong crowd. And I was only 18, for Christ's sake. That's *way* too young. So I'd sit on the can and rub my head. I'd look up at the ceiling but was always afraid to ask "why?" in case someone actually answered and told me what I really didn't want to hear, maybe something I'd suppressed like I really *did* screw a monkey or hang a cat. It wasn't fair, but I never said that. Nope. I just sat there until I didn't have enough liquid in my body to either bleed or cry.

One time I got the big four-cupper measuring cup out and let my nose bleed into it to see how much I was losing. I had seen the newsreels of the hockey player whose throat was slashed by a blade and he was bleeding all over the ice in buckets and he lost something like four or five pints before he got something like a hundred stitches to save his life. The most I ever got out of my nose and ears was, like, a half a cup, and the blood out of my ass wasn't a gusher, or anything, so I knew I wasn't going to die. The hockey player was on his feet and practicing with the team, like, four days later, so I also know the body refills fast.

It got better after about the third time. By then, I had it down to a routine. I bought Kleenex by the caseload, and toilet paper, too. I'd just strip off my clothes and start stuffing all the openings I had, even if they hadn't erupted yet, just in case. One day I looked in the mirror and I'd done an especially fine job of stuffing. The Kleenex was coming out my nose like I had walrus tusks, out of my ears like one of those old men sprouting hair like straw, and a wad out my ass like I was a bunny rabbit. I couldn't help it, I laughed like a balloon bursting, so hard one wad came popping out of my nose like a pea blown from a straw, and splattered on the mirror the way zombies explode when they're shot in the head. It made me laugh harder. I stuffed some more Kleenex into the nostril and pinched my nose so it wouldn't fly out again and one of the ear pieces dropped out. It probably had nothing to do with the laughing but out it came and now I was in full screaming, sink-pounding fits, until I started to cough and had to sit down on the can and, yup, you guessed it. So there I was until I almost couldn't breathe and my stomach muscles were killing me. I began to calm down, breath deeply, and then it all washed over me again and there I was, wondering why this was happening to me

The other thing about this "little diary". . . The Doc said I should take notes and then, later, when I had time, to flesh it out. He used that term: "flesh it out." Only a doctor would say that with a straight face, eh? But that's what I have been doing, which is why this reads (I hope) more like a story than a bunch of notes: "Casino, lights, whirling, neon, little old ladies in pyjamas."

The Doc said the whole exercise would be "useful" but he didn't say for whom. It has been for me, I suppose, especially 'fleshing it out' because I've crammed a lot into a few weeks and it's been fun to put it down and think about it in such detail. I might never have thought back on all this if I hadn't taken his advice and jotted stuff down.

Then again, the only other person to whom this might be "useful" would be *him*. I'd just be an unpaid dupe. He asked patients to write stuff down so he could use it in the research he was doing about "the five stages of grief." That was creepy to hear. The word grief, that is. He said I would go through these stages, maybe not all of them, but some, and he and his colleagues were studying how people of different ages cope with them. Denial, anger, depression, pleading and acceptance. He said not everyone wanted to be part of it, and I didn't have to jot down everything "as honestly as you can," but he would appreciate it. I said would, but only to get out of there so I didn't have to hear him blather on about his work any longer.

When I thought about it later, though, it pissed me off. I had been dragged there to talk about my health but what my health turned out to be was actually a great opportunity for this quack to use me to win the Nobel Prize without paying or even acknowledging me because he expected I'd be dead. I imagined he'd phone up one day and ask how my diary was going but he never did.

I don't really know whether it was because I said I would, even though I told myself I wouldn't, but I bought a steno pad and started the diary you're reading. I figured I might be off base about this. After all, he couldn't have used *all* his patients for this kind of stuff, could he?

"You have about ten days to live, Mr. Therapondis. Write fast please."

In light of the distraction it's given me, especially as I flesh it out for you now, I've decided to think better of him.

CHAPTER TWELVE

In retrospect, I think I was still hung over a bit the next day but I felt so much better that I started planning what to do next. Actually, I *knew* what I had to do, if Abdul was right about the afterlife and all. Get laid. But how, that was another matter.

I couldn't just go back to school and hit on the sluttiest girl there. Too many questions would have to be answered and besides, even if I were honest about it, I didn't want that mercy fuck, I wanted a real one, an adult fuck, a porn star fuck, and the only way I was going to get that without spending too much time was to rent it. But how I was going to do that was a bit tricky.

I knew hookers patrolled the lower part of Church Street, under the spires of the United and Catholic cathedrals, and St. James south on the other side of the street, and I knew it was night when they cruised there, but how to approach them and how much to pay, and where the deed would be done, well, those were all mysteries. Disease was beside the point; gonorrhea, syphilis, even AIDS was not an issue, given my apparent situation. But I'd have to come up with a strategy and the best one I could come up with was to go down there and observe, maybe even target a good-looking one, and go from there. So off I went. A little early.

Okay, so I was anxious. A lot anxious. It was still light out when I got there, so I sat on one of the church benches and watched the people. It's not as interesting as you might think. If you're not into beggars, or ladies who feed pigeons, or the occasional priest wandering around the grounds looking lost, really lost, then there's not much to see. And it takes an eternity to get dark. The waiting must drive cat burglars crazy.

Across the street, old Ivan's shop was boarded up and the sight of it made my stomach ache so I thought maybe I'd put Ivan's art to use. I wandered down Church until I spotted this tavern on the corner decked out in shamrocks and green and yellow signs. You could tell it was an old-fashioned tavern because it didn't have any windows. The old ones don't. They're like cocoons. The people inside don't want to be seen in there and they don't want to look out on life.

Now I knew about taverns. Taverns were all about beer and everyone my age drinks beer. One of the first times I ever went into a tavern, a guy about 30 years old overheard me and my friends talking shit about beer and the best places to find it. This guy – I can't remember his name – was sitting at the next table and his right hand seemed paralyzed into a cup shape that fit perfectly around the middle of a draft glass. Even when he wasn't holding a glass, it still looked like an ice cream scoop. In other words, he was an expert and taught us well as we bought him as many rounds as it took to squeeze his knowledge bank dry.

The draft room down Church was an old, dark, hardwood coffin of a place with a tin ceiling, beer-bleached floors, heavy tables and, stretching down the left side of the room, a long, fat, round-lipped, waxed, oak slab of a bar with a line of high stools in front of it. At the back of the room, men with boot polish hair and stained white aprons poured draft into glasses designed to be grabbed and held safely by fleshy hands, thumb or no thumb. No trust is permitted in a tavern.

No trust is given. Little white lines are painted near the rims of the draft glasses and mugs so everyone knows they are getting the same amount each time. In a restaurant there are no little white lines; wine is poured for profit margin more than a licensing law and the government knows profit is a better enforcer.

In a lot of taverns, the draft beer may hit the line every time but patrons don't get much of a choice as to what kind of draft is drawn. It's usually from the company that kicks back the most to the owner. It's only technically illegal and never enforced unless you hang a municipal election sign on the walls. For every politician an owner backs, there are three municipal licence inspectors who hate the meddling bastard. Politics, as a result, is not played by owners of old-style taverns and draft halls.

Pickled eggs in a big jar are always on display in a true tavern, as opposed to a chain wannabe where the restrooms are always cleaner. You want the grey ones, not the pristine white ones. The pristine ones are just freshly peeled hard-boiled eggs dropped in salted vinegar in a jar and delivered from a restaurant supplier. They don't make your mouth pucker, they don't reek of sulphur and above all, they don't go with draft beer. They're for show only, an atmospheric decoration planted by some effete corporate concept idiot who had never spilled a beer on a well-worn floor of a real draft hall in his life. The grey pickled eggs, however, mean the place is genuine. These are old eggs, leftover eggs, hard-boiled and bottled with a secret homemade brine cooked up in the back room and left for a few weeks before being brought out and sold. Those eggs stain your brain and bubble in your mouth with the beer. And the darker and greyer the better. Pickled eggs and cheap scratchy toilet paper are two signs of the real deal in taverns.

The pickled eggs were grey in this one and it made my heart flutter. I sat down at one of the tables and, sure enough, another telltale sign of authenticity manifested itself; the table didn't wobble on uneven legs like almost all restaurant tables do. These tables had been there for so long, and were so heavy, they were rooted in the floor. This was all very comforting.

About six guys were knocking back the beer, three at one table, two at another and a lone guy at the bar. The lone guy was interesting. He was weaving from side to side and forward and back as he sat on the stool and eventually, after I'd had two drafts, tipped back and fell right off the stool, cracking down on the floor with slow-motion grace. A waiter walked by, leaned over and said, "you okay, Walter?" Walter didn't move at first but then nodded from the floor and the waiter walked off, as if nothing had happened. I didn't know whether to get up and help the poor guy or laugh, but I did neither, I just watched this little soap opera pan out. About a minute later, this Walter guy rolled over onto his knees, stayed quietly like a pointer for about 30 seconds, reared himself up, grabbed the stool, whirled around and sat down at the bar again. With a steady hand, he grasped the draft glass in front of him and tipped it up. The bartender came over, looked at him like a doctor and said, "you okay, Walter?" Walter nodded and the bartender sauntered off to the pumps at the far end. No one else in the place paid the slightest attention to this whole scene. The three guys down the way just kept talking and drinking and so too did the two at the other table. I was the only one who seemed to be aware that Walter was even in the place.

"What's with that guy?" I asked the waiter when he came over to offer me a couple more beers.

"That's Walter," he said, "lives upstairs. He's a clown."

"Yeah, a real clown," I said.

"Yup," the waiter said, "a real clown." He put two drafts on the table. Walter wasn't weaving anymore, but he seemed to have nailed himself to the bar through the clothes on his arms. I watched him for awhile and couldn't stand it any longer. Normally, I wouldn't have done it because, well, I'm 18 and someone like that was weird and probably wouldn't mean much to me in life. But for some reason now – and probably because I'd knocked back those drafts pretty fast – I had to know. I took my beer and sat down on the stool beside him.

I didn't look at his face, like I was being nonchalant, or something, but eventually I turned and he was grinning at me.

"Oh, hi," I said.

"Hello," he said. His voice was strong, not watery like you'd expect a drunk's to be. "You new around here?"

"Ah, yeah, just dropped in for a few," I said.

"You're just a kid."

"I'm old enough."

"We're all old enough," he said, "it's just whether you're *old* enough, if you know what I mean."

I shook my head.

"Chronology doesn't mean a thing," he said. "If you're sixteen, the government says you can kill yourself in a car but not with cigarettes or booze. That's chronology for ya. And if you're eighteen, you can screw a 15-year-old and it's okay, but if you're twenty-one and screw the 15-year-old, you're a rapist. That, too, is chronology. Chronology is crap. For instance, I'll bet you're sixteen or seventeen and you're drinking in here where you have to be nineteen."

"I'm not, I'm twenty-one, and I can prove it," I said. I was a bit alarmed by this guy. I took out my ID and showed him. He looked at it and smiled.

"Too bad about Ivan," he said. "It's okay, everyone knew him, everyone liked him, and he sent whatever kid came through his door over here to test drive his work. Everyone knew he sent them here, the owners knew the ID was bogus but great. They needed the business, Ivan gave them some, and they went along with it. Everyone was a winner. Chronologies be damned."

I shook my head and took a long sip of the beer. I didn't know what to say.

"I was right, wasn't I?"

I looked at him again and nodded. "The cops shot him, right?"

"Oh, no, they knew Ivan, too," Walter said. "One of the jewelry robbers was running around the back, saw Ivan hightailing it out the door and dropped him with one shot, and Isaac with the second. A good thing the cops were there, actually, because they blew that bastard away right then and there. Justifiable homicide, I'd say. Actually, everybody said that. No way was anyone going to rat on the cop. We all know him and he's a good guy. We all gave him the nod, the old tip of the cap, when we saw him again. He knew he was okay with us, and we were the only ones who knew. But I am right, right? That's Ivan's work."

I nodded again, admired the workmanship once more and then put it back in my wallet.

"Recent?" Walter asked.

"I was there when it happened. I saw it. Not the Ivan and Isaac part. Ivan had just given it to me when they ran in the back door and out the front." As soon as I said it, I started to panic. I could see it in Walter's eyes. He knew. And if he didn't know then, he was going to figure it out that I had the gold.

"You didn't go to the cops?"

"No, no, I didn't," I said.

"You're not going to, are you?"

"No, no," I said.

"You're okay, then, kid. No use in opening that can of worms. And if you're not going to talk about this to anyone, I'm not going to ask you any questions about it, okay?"

"Fine by me," I said.

"And when I see that cop, I can tell him everything is cool, right? I mean, he knows someone else is out there with information. All the cops do. But they can't find him, and they're a bit worried that person might show up one day and embarrass them. But if that person isn't going to show up . . ."

"That person is *not* going to show up," I said.

"They'll be really happy to hear that," Walter said. "You're okay, kid." Walter pried the nail out of one of his arms, raised his hand and yelled "Gerald! Bring my friend here a draft on me!"

"Thanks, I said, "but I may have had enough."

"Never enough, my boy. Never enough."

"But maybe I should buy you one?"

"If you like, but first we'll drink on me." Gerald whacked down two more foamy glasses in front of us. Walter reached into his pocket and pulled out a wad of bills, peeled off a five spot and gave it to the barman. There must have been a couple of hundred in the roll.

"Cheers," I said, and raised my glass. "Cheers," said Walter. I watched him tip it back and drain it in three gulps. This was getting confusing.

"Walter, I don't want to be nosey, but, ah, what do you do?"

"Oh, I'm just a clown," he said.

"Yeah, that's what the waiter said, a real clown."

"It's true. A real clown," he said.

I let this sink in. It was getting the better of me and I had to know for some reason, like it was life and death, and maybe it was, given the fact Walter now knew I was involved in the Ivan incident and the cops were looking for me, which gave me the creeps. "No, seriously, what do you do?"

Walter looked at me with a cockeyed grin on his face, a big one. He then put his hand in his pocket and pulled out two balloons, which he quickly blew up and twisted into a dog, as easily as if he were simply slipping on some winter gloves. He handed it over to me, still with that grin, tipped his head, and an imaginary cap, and then went back to the draft he had left on the bar.

"Holy, shit," I said.

"What did you think I was?"

"Not a real clown. I mean, how many times in life do you meet a real clown?"

"Everyone meets a clown at some time or other. We go way back," he said. "Not just here, you know. Everywhere. Clowns performed for the ancient Pharaohs in Egypt, Cortez stole Montezuma's clown in Mexico and gave him to the Pope, even Uncle Sam was a clown before he began recruiting for American wars. I'll bet you went to half a dozen birthday parties as a kid where a clown like me twisted balloons and squirted you with a daisy."

I nodded and took a swig.

"Like they say, 'we're everywhere, we're everywhere!' " He was looking at me for some reaction.

"So, you're a clown here. For kids?"

"Yup. And I did a gig for General Motors yesterday."

"General Motors?"

"The Auto Show. Put the big floppy feet on, I guess to show people you could get into one of their minivans even if you've got big feet. I didn't ask. GM pays well. Then I entertained the kids as the sales guys hit on the fathers."

"That's funny."

"I thought so." When he said this, he started to sway on his stool again. First he swayed forward and back and then, as if he were attached to the ceiling with a string, started swinging around in circles, then sideways. I was about to grab him when he stopped altogether. I'd just let out a sigh of relief when he lurched backwards off the stool and went crashing to the floor.

"Jesus Christ!" I yelled. "Help. Somebody help me." I jumped off my own stool and knelt down beside Walter. He looked up at me with blinking eyes A waiter came by and stood over us.

"He's okay, aren't you, Walter?" he asked. Walter looked at him and smiled back.

"What the hell is going on?" I asked the waiter.

"Plate in his head," he said. "He's okay. He hits the plate when he goes down and bounces right back up."

"That right, Walter?"

Walter smiled and then slowly, on his own, rolled over to the dog position, waited, and then hauled himself back onto his stool. Gerald had put another draft in front of his seat. I was shaking when I sat down again. "God, that scared the shit out of me," I said. And he smiled. It was if he couldn't speak.

"He won't say anything for a while," Gerald said. "Can't. Don't know why. He'll come around again in a few seconds, though. Want another draft?" I shook my head and looked at my watch. It was already 10:00 p.m. I'd been there for a couple of hours and hadn't even noticed. I clapped Walter on the shoulder. "You okay, really? I gotta go but I won't if you're not okay." Walter raised his hand and with a surprisingly fluid wrist, shooed me away. He mouthed, "thanks," but didn't actually say it. I hesitated, but then climbed down and walked outside. I stood there on the stoop looking up and down the street, but not really thinking about anything except Walter crashing down off that stool. *Jeezes*, I thought, *that was weird.*

I looked at my watch again and then scanned the area. I wasn't sure I was up to this, after what I'd just seen, so I walked up the street again, went into the park and sat down on one of the church benches for quite awhile. No harm in just watching, was there?

Church Street had changed in just a few hours. I thought I saw a few hookers walking down the street, short skirts, smoking, but they kept walking quickly and then turned east toward Jarvis Street. All the pawn shops across the street still had their front lights on but chain grates and fences boxed them in; the lights were on but nobody was home. The cars, which hours before were crushing each other to get where they were going north of there, were now moving south just as slowly but with no one blocking them, the drivers' heads looking out the side windows, then turning east at the lights in the same direction the girls walked. It looked like a sign to me so I got up and hoofed it east.

Jarvis is a bit dark over there at night. The street is five lanes wide and the city regulates the centre line with either a red "X," meaning don't go there, or a green "Y," meaning you can drive in that lane. This night, the green light was for the southbound traffic and cars were screaming down the centre and the lane right next to it but crawling along the lane nearest the curb. From my vantage point, on the south-west corner, I could see a bunch of girls waiting for a bus outside the Sears building. They were, as one of my friends would describe them, "skanky" with short skirts and visible stockings going all the way up and despite the cool weather, dressed rather scantily. I know, I know, they were hookers to you, but to me at first sight they looked like office girls waiting for the bus, except I eventually realized no buses come down Jarvis Street and the cars crawling on the curb lane were trolling for these girls. I have to tell you, though, my heart sank a little. I was no expert but these girls reeked of disease and cheap blow jobs and even though my initial impetus was for just this moment, they were, well, too skanky even for me, despite the beer under my belt. I thought the disease part was irrelevant, but when I looked at them on the sidewalk, all I could think about was intimate parts falling off in great oozing puddles.

As a study in sociological goings-on, however, they were pretty interesting. For one thing, they all seemed to smoke. Now, I'm no moralist but smoking is just plain stupid, it reeks and it almost got Saul Shloman killed at camp. I think I told you that. I had kissed a few girls who smoked and when the thrill wore off, all I was left with was the taste of that smoke.

For another thing, the girls on Jarvis seemed to have a pecking order. When a car pulled up, they didn't all leap at the car.

One would go poke her head through the window and either get in or back off, and if the latter, another would approach and talk to whomever. It all seemed pretty democratic. At one point a car pulled up and a girl got out of the passenger side. What was different about her was she was fairly decent looking, not as slutty as the others. And she didn't talk to the bus stop ladies; she walked a bit south, toward me more, and stood by herself. She seemed to be turned out well, her hair didn't go all over the place or was slicked down with hair gel, and her lipstick wasn't florescent, but subdued. Now, maybe that was because the rest of her lipstick was now encircling some guy's cock, I don't know, but her lips looked more like Lindsay Lohan rather than bright red Cindy Crawford, not that Cindy Crawford is a hooker, although wouldn't *that* be something?

About two minutes later, another car pulled up and disgorged another girl, and this one, too, was fairly decent looking, she didn't talk to the bus stop broads either and she, too, walked toward me and stopped to talk to the Lindsay-Lohan-lips hooker. Now I had a theoretical choice, and I began to get a little excited. Maybe this was going to turn out okay after all. I started ruminating what my best lines should be. I imagined approaching them, like James Bomb again maybe, and saying something that would make them toss their heads in laughter and then fight over me, with a little decorum of course, as to who would do me and where. One would win, take my arm, lead me to a nice room somewhere, where she would initiate me into the world of manhood. And just when I started walking toward them, mumbling to myself the opening pick-up line, I ran right into another girl who had appeared from nowhere and I nearly lost my beer right there. This one was simply gorgeous. A knock out, Beautiful. Stunning. Subdued. Classy. Almost preppy. "Can I buy you a drink?" I said, actually just saying what I was going to say to the other girls, but it just came out and she looked at me with her mouth slightly open, showing fabulous teeth, and then her eyes sort of crinkled up a little, as if she were smiling in her brain, and she just stared at me.

"I beg your pardon?" she said.

"Can I, ah, like, buy you a drink?" I said again. And again she just looked at me like she was studying a wacko modern painting and trying to figure what it was supposed to mean. She looked me up and down. At one point she took a step back to see all of me, from my Weejuns to the throat of my Polo shirt under the blue blazer.

"How old are you?" she asked.

"Twenty-one. Want to see my ID?" I said, maybe too fast.

"Twenty-one, eh? I'm twenty-one and you don't look as old as I do," she said.

"I can prove it," I said, and started to pull my wallet out of my pocket. She put her hand up like a traffic cop to stop me.

"No, no, I'm sure you can prove it," she said, and then paused again. "You've never picked up a hooker, have you?"

I didn't have a clue what to say. I just stood there, my mind racing to come up with something but nothing was about to come out.

"I thought so," she said. "Tell you what, you can buy me a drink but nothing else, okay? And it's going to cost you a lot of money. You've got money, I trust?" I nodded and began to pull out my wallet again, but once more she put her hand up. "Okay," she said, "follow me. You got a car?" I shook my head. "We'll take mine, then." She walked across the street at the lights and led me into a small parking lot where she pulled a bunch of keys from her purse, made a car go "beep, beep" and the headlights flash, and she got into the driver's side of a BMW convertible. I got into the red leather passenger seat. I had struck the virtual gold mine. I was going for a ride, in more ways than I had ever dreamed was possible.

This girl drove like a race car driver. She moved through the gears like a pastry chef smoothly squeezing initials on a birthday cake from a plastic bottle, and she took it to almost the red line with every shift. In about two seconds – okay, it was longer than that but I was holding my breath for most of it – she was screaming to a stop in front of an apartment portico and a doorman was helping her out of the car. Dammit, she was taking me home. I really had hit the jackpot! I followed her into the front and almost fainted at the sight of this girl's perfect ass under what appeared to be very much like fabric my mother would buy at Holt's. In other words, firm and expensive. My head was swimming when we walked into a large dining room and I realized we were in a restaurant.

"You *do* have money on you, right?" she asked. I nodded. I had about five hundred bucks. She smiled at the guy behind the dimly lit stand at the door, and he led us to a table by a huge window that looked south over the city sparkling below and beyond. The view was vast and deep.

"You are not only going to buy me a drink, but you are going to buy me dinner because I'm starving. Then we're going to talk a little and then you are going to go away," she said. I guess from my expression she understood my confusion. "You are *not* twenty-one, so let's get that out of the way. I'd say you were about seventeen, eighteen at the very most, and you might very well be sixteen, which I think would make you illegal in more ways than I can think," she said. "Second, I was right about you never picking up a street girl before, right?" I nodded. "Third, you've got to think this over very carefully, preferably for a day, and then decide whether you want to endanger yourself so much. And lastly, you should be realistic about how much someone like me costs."

I blinked, probably too quickly, too much. "Okay," I said. "But I'm not."

"Not what?"

"Sixteen."

"Okay, so how old are you?"

"Older."

"But still a virgin, right?"

I probably blushed. I felt wet under the arms.

"That's okay Sweetie," she said, "It's kinda nice to see someone still innocent these days." She leaned across the table and grasped my hand. I thought I would faint. Her hand was so soft, her touch so gentle, and her eyes, well, her eyes were almost moist. I felt a connection, unlike anything I have felt before. I swear, it was magic. I would have followed this girl into the pits of hell at that moment.

"Now order," she said, and opened the menu.

The whole menu was a blur. I couldn't concentrate on a thing. When the waiter first appeared, the girl ordered a glass of white wine for both of us. When he appeared later to take the order, she said, "he'll have the cold smoked salmon to start and the filet medium rare for the main, and I'll have the calamari and the venison. And you pick the red for the mains." He smiled and left.

"So, what do you want to tell me about yourself?" she asked. I felt like such a doofus. I couldn't speak in front of her. I was spinning.

"I don't know, what would you like to know?"

"You've never been here before, right?"

"Right."

"But you live around here, don't you?"

"No, actually, I don't. At least I don't think so. Where are we?"

"Scaramouche. Avenue Road, below St. Clair, above Yorkville."

"Oh, I think I've heard of it," I said. And I think I had.

"So you don't go to the private schools around here, so you don't live in Forest Hill. You live south or north of here?"

"South."

"So Rosedale?"

"How'd you know that?"

"Weejens, Polo shirt, blue blazer. That hair cut."

"Oh," I said.

"What beats me, though is the virgin status," she said, "you're not a bad looking kid. In a few years you are going to be handsome, really. I'd of thought some private school girl would have jumped you years ago. Never mind. My gain, I suppose."

The waiter brought the first courses. The smoked salmon came with these potato chips that you couldn't really call chips, with avocado and a sharp lemony jelly and sour cream. I've had smoked salmon before, on a bagel with cream cheese, but I made a mental note between bites to see if I could make this at home somehow. The wine wasn't sweet at all, but not mouth-puckering, either. And it gave me a bit of a glow on top of the draft buzz.

The filet mignon was so tender you could cut it with a fork. And it had this dark beefy sauce that stuck to the roof of my mouth with this lasting taste that seemed to breathe out my nose at the same time. The red wine made me feel as if I were melting into the seat as I looked out over the city. At this point, I couldn't have been more relaxed or, what's the word? Contented. Not laid, but just about as happy and relieved somehow.

We didn't talk much as we ate. Her choice, actually. She watched when I started my meal. When I tried to make conversation, she put her hand up just like she did downtown and said, "Don't think. Do.

"If you have the choice of pleasure and pain, take the pleasure, but learn to enjoy it to the fullest so you won't regret ignoring the painful path you should have taken to please everyone else. Learn to enjoy it. Savor each bite and take little bites. Chew softly. Despite what you've been told, chew with your mouth open. Part your lips just slightly so you can breathe in as you eat. The flavor will be intensified. The same is true with the wine. It needs air to bring it to life. You have to breathe and smell food and wine. Smell is the most important and complex part of taste. Of all your senses, actually." She picked up her fork and demonstrated with her dinner.

"You're not really alive if you can't smell. You're just imagining life," she said.

The bill came as I finished a glass of cognac, a liqueur that burned my mouth like scotch but singed my nose hairs, too. It was smooth and made my brain warm. What was freaky was when she ordered it, she said the same thing my father did. She said, "since you've never had a cognac before, you should start with the very best so you can rate all the others from then on." When it came, the waiter gave it to her, not me. They smiled at each other. She held it in both palms, swirling it around in front of her face, sniffing it several times, and then handed it to me like she was cupping my balls. When I thought about it, and took the glass and realized how hot her hands were, I almost passed out. I finished it, my brain was bubbling and I slapped down three hundred dollars for the meal without a second thought.

Her car was waiting by the front door. She looked at me when the guy opened the door and even I knew what I had to do. I gave him a twenty, she smiled, we got in and she headed downtown again as fast as we had arrived. When we got to the corner where we met, she stopped the car. "Okay, Sweetie. Think about it tonight. If you want to continue, I'll be at the bar in the Four Seasons' Hotel tomorrow night – you know where that is? – between eight and eight thirty. Come alone and bring twenty-five hundred dollars."

My eyes must have doubled in size.

"I told you I was expensive. How much did you think this was going to cost?"

"I, ah, don't know exactly."

"Exactly twenty-five hundred dollars. You know, Sweetie, someone like me gets a thousand an hour but we're going to make a night of it, you and me. We are going to do this right and it will be worth every penny. So be there or not, it doesn't matter to me, but if you are going to be there, be on time. Think about it. Long and hard. Bye bye." She reached over my lap, brushed against my groin giving me a jolt in the process, opened the door and shooed me away. I left the car as meekly as I had entered a few hours before and she squealed off, revving the motor to the red line. The BMW tore up Jarvis. As I stood there, all I could do was think about how beautiful she was, how she had touched my hand in the restaurant, how she had accidently brushed my lap, and eventually, what the hell was I going to do? I needed to think. So I walked over to the tavern again.

Gerard was leaning way over the bar and looking down. A couple of waiters and about five guys were standing around. "Walter? Walter? You all right?" I heard someone ask. I made my way in, looked through the throng, and there was Walter, flat on his back, but this time not moving or blinking or anything.

CHAPTER THIRTEEN

G erard pushed Walter's shoulder to see if he moved. "Is he dead?" I asked.

"Nah, he's just out," he said, looking up at me. "But we gotta get him upstairs. Give Henry here some help. We're short-staffed tonight."

The crowd around Walter drew back and Henry, one of the waiters, grabbed Walter under the armpits and dragged him to the middle of the floor. He then motioned to me with his head to grab his feet, which I did, not because I wanted to touch Walter in any way, but because I thought I had no choice. Henry then backed out the side door with me bringing up the rear, literally, until we were in a hall with a high, oak, wide staircase leading to a dimly lit hall. We hauled old Walter upstairs and then to a door that Henry kicked open and we went inside to a room about the size of a two-car garage. Henry was grunting. We carried Walter to a bulky matted cloth reclining chair, a mechanical farting chair really, where Henry draped him into the seat, made sure his ass was firmly in place and his head against the chair's back. He took his left arm and stretched it across his leg and put the remote control in his hand pointed at the television to the right of the chair it. Henry stepped to the set and manually turned it on. The Comedy channel popped to life.

"Okay, we're done," Henry said. "We can go."

"And just leave him like that?"

"Sure, sure. He's gonna be fine. He wake up eventually. Oh yeah . . ." he said and marched back to the far end where a refrigerator, sink and a small gas stove were set against the wall. He opened the fridge, looked inside and then shut the door. Then he looked into a cupboard and shut that, too. "It's okay," he said. "Walt's got some cereal."

"That's okay?"

"Sure, sure. He probably won't be down for breakfast tomorrow so we make sure he got somethin' to eat. He got milk and cereal. He'll be okay. We can go."

"Don't you think it'd be wise to make sure he doesn't die, or something?"

"He'll be fine, but you can stay if you want. He no mind." And Henry left, shutting the door almost quietly, as if he might wake up Walter.

The room was almost square, with that all-in-one room effect, the kitchen against the far wall, a bed to Walter's left against the other wall, a walled-in cupboard-like room between the two, which I discovered was a fairly filthy washroom with a toilet, sink and shower, and a large window to his right that overlooked the front of the hotel and the street. I knew it was the front because the neon sign was right out front of his window and it glowed red, just like in really bad movies. By the front door a tall armoire was tilting to one side, its door partially open to reveal a few jackets and pants on hangers with two drawers below. On a coat rack hanger screwed to the side was a full clown's suit and just below it, a pair of those long floppy shoes.

The television was old but a cable snaked across the floor and was attached to a box, which meant Walter had his cable in an upgrade mode. As for Walter, he was snoring through an old Marx Brothers' movie, *A Day at The Races*.

Walter moaned and moved his head to the other side of the chair back so I knew he was alive, just as Henry said, so I decided I could go. But as I turned to the door, Walter spoke and scared the hell out of me. Until then, it had been really really quiet in the room.

"Hey kid," he said, "thanks for bringing me up here."

"No, not at all. Glad I could help . . . you okay?"

"Absolutely. Need a nap now and then," he said, and laughed.

From the dead to the quick in a flash. Walter was wide awake and as lucid as I was. Amazing. "Wow," was all I could manage.

"Hey, you want a drink?" he asked.

"Ah, nah, I think I'm good," I said.

"No one's good," he said. "Not a soul on earth, except for kids. But you can get me one, then." Walter pointed at a small table beside the window. I hadn't noticed it before. On it was a crystal decanter full of a deep red liquid, and beside it four crystal glasses, just like ones my grandmother used to have, you know, with the flowery cuts on the outside of the glass like palm fronds around Easter, and the skinny lip that sings if you rub your wetted finger around the edge? Like those. I pointed at them. Walter nodded. So I poured him a half glass and handed it over.

"Sure you don't want a drink?" he asked again. "It's vintage port, 16-years-old. Very nice. Sweet, perfect with blue cheese, although one should really drink Tawny with Stilton but I rarely have the cheese so I buy the vintage stuff for sipping at night."

I watched him sip the port. He wacked back the draft downstairs but here, in his room, he tipped the port back like an octogenarian connoisseur. Then he looked at it through the glass as if he were examining some jewel.

"I don't mean to be rude or nosey but how can you do that? I mean, they just found you passed out downstairs and here you are, perfect, drinking some more and you don't sound a bit, you know, plastered, or anything?"

"I'm not," he said. "You drink as much as me for as long as I have and you never show it. As for the passed out bit, well, that's just the plate in my head; it switches my brain off and on once in awhile. I just wish I knew when the switch was going to be pulled. Then I could warn people around me it was going to happen. And I wish I would know beforehand when the switch was going to be off for longer than usual. Scares the shit out of some people. Not the guys downstairs, though. That's why I live here. They're used to it and they know they can just bring me up here and they don't have to worry about me. Good guys, those guys. Never let me down yet."

I didn't really know what to make of this. "But I've seen you fall off the stool downstairs. That's gotta hurt."

"Nah. Don't feel a thing, really. I'm switched off when I hit, so it's like being under anaesthetic. Then I wake up almost always straight away. I can't speak for a bit, and I can't move much. I think it's a wiring thing. It takes a few minutes for the wires to reconnect. But when I start feeling some movement, I can roll over on my hands and knees and that seems to help. Then I can haul myself up. After awhile, I get my voice back again. End of story."

"Until you don't wake up."

"Yeah, that's true, but then the guys get me up here again."

"What happens during the day, though? I mean, what happens if it happens when you're shopping or out for a walk?"

"Never does. Never during the daylight. Never when I'm outside this place, actually. It all started here and it stops here, too. Can't explain it. Just doesn't. Weird, huh?"

"I'll say."

"Nope, which is why I never worry when I work. I'd hate it if I scared the kids. I'd quit the job. Kids are the greatest and I'm a clown and clowns may scare some kids but not because we're clowns but because we're strange and anything strange scares some kids. Most kids are innocent, fearless, loved and secure and clowns don't scare them at all." Walter took another sip, smacked his lips, looked through the liquid and smiled. "And besides, I never drink when I'm working. Never. I'm just like a pilot. If I've got a gig, I won't drink for at least 24 hours before. Not because I would be jittery or out of control – I can do the routine with my eyes closed – but because I don't want to smell of alcohol. I'm flawed because I'm an adult. But I don't want to expose the kids to real-life flaws as a clown. Clowns should be happy, sad and clean all at the same time."

"Sad?"

"Absolutely. All clowns are sad. You can't be happy, and especially not funny, all the time."

"Why not?"

"That's not a kid's life. No kid is happy *all* the time. And funny people are only good to be around if they're funny all the time. And you can't be funny all the time. Not even the proverbial Christmas uncle."

"Who?"

"You know, the uncle who comes to visit once a year at Christmas and is *so* funny! Then one year he comes and he's not funny because he's had a heart attack or his wife has left him or he blew his foot off in a hunting accident. And he's not funny that year and it couldn't be a bigger downer and no one wants to be around him. You're just a kid yourself but your balls have dropped so you should know this. The guy who's the clown in school, a friend of yours, maybe even you yourself. And all the pretty girls love this guy because he's *so* funny. You ask any girl what she wants in a boyfriend and every one of them says, "I want someone who can make me laugh." That's absolute bullshit. They love this guy because he's funny and easy to be around but the second, the *instant,* he's not funny anymore, the girl gets bored and leaves. You see, he can't be funny all the time anymore. She can't count on it anymore. But the bad boy? The hard ass, cruel bastard boyfriend, the dangerous one? Well, the girl knows he's bad ass and dangerous, but then he can change on the outside and be nice to the girl, and that makes the girl think she has

mellowed him, but she also knows that just below the surface, this guy can turn on her at any time. If he doesn't, it's because of her. If he does, it's his true nature coming out again and she has to tame it again, to reassert her power. There's no way to make a guy funny anymore, though. That's lost." Walter took another sip before continuing.

"It's not natural to be funny all the time, not for you and not for the funny guy. You always hear about the comics who kill themselves. They can't stand being funny all the time. In fact, very few of them are funny in private. They're tortured. No one is funny all the time. Kids' parents certainly aren't. They can be loving and supportive and kind, although kids don't know kind from allowance-giver, and once in awhile they're funny. But that's rare. The world isn't funny to kids. Kids are cruel to other kids. Kids shit their pants and wet their beds at the most inconvenient times. They fall down and scrape their knees and little girls get tied to rose bushes by little boys who think they're playing games but are really trying to show the girls they like them. Life is confusing, painful and unjust to kids growing up. That's just the way it is. Good clowns are always two things: physically as big as parents and they have a frown painted on their faces. So when a clown comes into their homes, he does funny stupid things, and makes balloons and cracks silly jokes and sings weird songs. He's working in that space between the frown where the kids don't want to go and adults who create the frown. It's a safe place and the wider the gap is created, the better the clown is. And then there's a great clown, one who can pick out the kids who like clowns and kids who are afraid of them. Kids who ask all the questions like clowns. The afraid kids never ask a question. And I'm a great clown, kid, a great clown so I don't want to screw it up just because I can drink 35 draft beers and a bottle of port, fall off chairs and crack my head and come up laughing at the Marx Brothers." Walter pointed at the television. "I *love* this movie. It says it all!"

I could barely keep up. Here was this guy, who was unconscious on the floor of a sleazy tavern a few minutes before, being so bloody articulate now. In a few seconds he had given a philosophical dissertation about kids and humor, adolescent frustration and hormones, all while demonstrating an apparently deep appreciation of the finer things in life, to wit, vintage port. *I* didn't even know what the hell port was, and I had this book at home that probably told me all about it.

"Surprised?"

Now this guy was reading my mind! "Yeah, I suppose I am," I said.

"Have some port."

"Thanks but . . ."

"You driving tonight?"

"No, no . . ."

"Have a drink. I want to ask you a favor but I don't want to ask you without offering you a drop."

I looked at him. His eyes weren't exactly pleading but they weren't cold and demanding, either. I poured myself a small one and took a sip. It was sweet. It was also very smooth. It coated my mouth and when I breathed in, it breathed with me. It was damn good. Walter tipped his glass up in the air. "Cheers," he said. I raised my glass, repeated the greeting and took another sip.

"See the suit over there?" he said and pointed to the clown costume hanging on the side of the armoire. "I need it cleaned. I have a gig next week and if you look at the front, you'll see a stain. Little boy threw up his birthday cake on me. Along with the grape juice he chugged while waiting for his friends, probably scared shitless no one was going to show up at his party because he heard his mother talking to another mother about how that would be terrible. Just another parent projecting unrealistic fears upon their children without realizing what assholes they can be. Anyway, it's pure silk, worth a lot, probably three thousand now, and it can only be cleaned at one place I know of where they won't fade it, or shrink the damned thing, but the place has changed hands and these new guys . . . let's just say we didn't hit it off right away and I'd appreciate it if you took it yourself and asked that they be really, really careful and clean it for you. Not me. For you. Tell them you bought it from a dead clown's estate or something. Ask them how much it's going to cost and let me know. I'll give you the money before you pick it up. Just come back and let me know how much. It might take them awhile to clean it so I need to have it brought in now so it will be ready next week. Will you do that for me?" he asked and raised his glass again.

What could I say? "Sure." I took the last sip and took my glass into his kitchen and put it in the sink. He scribbled the name and address of the cleaners on a piece of paper from his pocket and handed it to me as I walked by. As I was taking the suit from the armoire hanger, my curiosity got the better of me again.

"Where's the plate?"

"In my head, of course."

"But where?"

He rubbed the back of his head, right where it hit the floor just before the rest of him.

"Why doesn't that kill you when you fall backwards then?"

"It's padded. I always seem to hit my head there. Don't know how but as they say, God protects clowns and drunks."

"I thought it was 'fools' and drunks."

"Fools, historically, are clowns."

"How'd it happen?"

"Fractured my skull so they took me to the hospital and operated on me to relieve the clot, but then my brain exploded ten days later when the area got infected and the puss literally ate my skull away. So they went back in and removed the bone and replaced it with a steel plate. And because the skin over the skull was half eaten away, too, they put a rubber membrane there to make it like the skin. When I fall on it now, I sort of bounce and it cushions the blow. When I fall back, it doesn't hurt, because there are no nerves there anymore, and I don't fracture my skull because it's steel."

"Jeezes . . . How'd you fracture your skull in the first place?" I asked.

"Fell off a bar stool backwards."

I picked up the clown suit and left.

CHAPTER FOURTEEN

In retrospect, the only good I could see from the beers and the port and the wine of the night before was that it slowed me down. Otherwise I would have had to run a marathon to stop the twitching. I didn't know how I was going to get through the day. I had decided at about six minutes after leaving Walter I *would* be in the Four Seasons' bar the next night, that I *would* meet that gorgeous girl again and that I *would* go through with it, no matter how much it cost or whether my dick fell off three days later. I had three missions: Get the money, drop the clown suit at the cleaners, and get down to that bar. Nothing else mattered. Nothing. It wasn't a big plan, would take 90 minutes on the outside, but I had *all god damned day* to do it. If I hadn't been so slow because of the booze, I would have gone mad.

I thought the money thing would be a problem — money is always a problem, right? — but I told the bank that I was going to buy a computer, cash down. The teller, and the teller's boss who had to initial the withdrawal slip, did it without even looking at the thing. Kids just buy computers every day, I guess, even if they're three thousand dollars.

I found the dry cleaners exactly where Walter said I would, but as soon as I walked in and showed the little guy what I needed cleaned, he got this squinty look in his eye.

"Where'd you get that from?" he asked.

Well, that stumped me because I knew I couldn't tell him because Walter said something had gone on between them, even if I didn't know what. But I took Walter's suggestion: "At an estate sale," I said.

"An estate sale?"

"When someone dies, they sell off all the things they don't want any more to get some cash, I guess."

The guy stopped squinting and he smiled a big one. "Dead? Someone died?"

"Yeah, I guess so, because I got this at an estate sale."

"Hey Manny," he called to the back of the store, "look what we got here!" Another little guy came out and took a look at the clown suit. "Hey, where'd you get that?" he asked. Before I could answer, the first little guy said, "Estate sale!" Now the second little guy smiled, but then he turned on me.

"How come you come here to get it cleaned?"

He almost had me, but I beat him to it once more: "There was an old ticket in the pocket," I said, "so I figured you'd know how to get the barf outta the thing, on the front, see?" I pointed to the stain.

Now both of them smiled big ones. "Yeah, yeah, we know how to clean this thing," Manny said. "Can't do it overnight or anything, though."

"That's okay, as long as I have it by the weekend because I'm going to a costume party, which is why I bought it in the first place. I don't want to look like a bum in the thing."

"A bum! A bum! You hear that, Manny?" They both started laughing so hard I thought they'd piss themselves. I couldn't help it, I started laughing, too. But I'm pretty sure we weren't laughing at the same thing.

When I left, I knew I had to ask Walter about what the hell was going on. I couldn't imagine. Actually, there were a lot of questions I wanted to ask Walter, like how he got so smart and where he was brought up, and who his family was, and whether he knew anything about this Paradise thing. But I'd have to wait because now I had to go home and get cleaned up and get ready for the Four Seasons and the earthly Paradise of, of, of, and . . . I realized I didn't even know her name. *Jeezes!* Maybe it was all a trick. Maybe it wasn't real. Maybe I'd go and she wouldn't be there. I started to sweat just thinking about how awful I would feel. I got the jumps in my stomach. When I got home, I thought maybe I'd puke at one point. This was terrible. It was a disaster of enormous proportions. And my stomach was still in knots when I got out of the taxi under the glittering lights of the entrance and was greeted by a doorman who gave me one of those all-knowing smiles one gives a lost kid looking for his mommy. I took one look at him and knew he was right. I *was* lost. I wanted to be found.

The bar was off to the left of the lobby and I could hear it before I saw it. And then I saw it and really got the willies. The place was martinis, wine and scotch on the rocks. There wasn't a beer in the bar. Nothing less than a carat and a half, either, 40ish women with hair swept back just enough to frame earlobes that glistered, dollar bills woven and dyed into dresses hemmed above the knees, and shoes that would be worn once and then thrown from balconies to Goodwill bins below. The men had shoes and haircuts that were polished and cut as they sat at their desks in offices 50 storeys up in front of walls of windows that were too hot from the sun for most of the day and boring without the sight of people passing by, although *that* would never cross their minds. The women were trying hard to look twenty. The men were looking for a twenty. And they found one sitting at a small table by the avenue window sipping on a glass of white wine. It was her. She was there. She was twenty-one, looking twenty, strong long legs, skin as smooth and taught as a Michelangelo marble, breasts beneath white Egyptian cotton free from the tyranny of harnesses, hair that was silk from tip to roots. She looked out the window at nothing in particular. Damn it, she glowed! A god damned halo wrapped around her head. If my stomach had twitched before, my lungs were now failing me.

"You made it," she said, a little smile forming, her eyes narrowing with them. "I really didn't know if you would."

"I did," I said.

"I can see that." She laughed. "You want something to drink?"

I looked around and saw scotch and martinis and heard ice cubes in crystal above the piped-in piano I was about to speak when she said, "No, not that. Have some wine. Pace yourself." She raised her hand and a waiter was there as if he had been hiding behind a plant ready to spring as soon as she spoke or an scintilla of her skin rippled. "Another glass of the New Zealand Sauvignon Blanc, Joey, and bring my friend here one, too, okay?" Then she plastered her eyes to mine.

"So, let's get some of the business out of the way immediately," she said. "You have the cash?"

"Yes."

"And you still want to go through with this?"

"Yes."

"Okay, but there are ground rules, all right?"

"Sure."

"I don't do some things. Just don't, so if I say 'no,' it *really* means, No."

"Understood," I said. She was scaring me a little with this direct approach.

"And you'll do *exactly* what I tell you to do, right?"

"Right. Fine," I said. I watched her face turn soft again.

"Okay, Sweetie, as long as we have that straight, we're going to have a great time tonight, I promise, and you won't forget it."

I nodded. It was all I could do. My stomach was churning again. My pants felt tight. I had worms in my legs. She raised her glass and I raised mine and I gulped down about half the wine at once without taking my eyes off hers. It was like I was in another part of my brain and all around it was black except for the light that was streaming straight into my eyeballs. It made the halo even more pronounced.

"So tell me, Sweetie. Just who *are* you?"

I don't know about you but when someone asks me who I am, it comes as a shock and I can't really answer. I mean, who *am* I? I could tell her that I'm an eighteen-year-old virgin with a death sentence over his head but *that* would be the antithesis of pillow talk, wouldn't it? I'd have to make something up but then I'd have to remember it and I'd screw up for sure. I'd never be able to last in an interrogation room at the cop shop. Just by *threatening* me with *sleep deprivation* they'd have me begging to tell them everything they wanted to know. I was right back with Chinky Chen again, that what you are is actually the impression you leave with others, but what sort of lasting impressions has an eighteen-year-old made? At least this eighteen-year-old. Not a whole lot. Which brings up the whole bit about what they're going to say at your funeral. Vacuous stuff for someone my age. 'He was such as fun guy, always full of life, couldn't have wanted a better friend.' What utter bullshit. All that means is that you've drifted through life just like everyone else and they haven't a clue what to say about you they couldn't say about themselves, if they thought about it, but they don't because they're not dead. It's like those interviews in locker rooms with hockey players who all say the same inane things. Why anyone wants to hear what these peons say night after night about how they play as a team and they play each period as it comes, and they give a hundred and ten percent every time they skate onto the ice, is an absolute mystery. Not one of them has any insight into what the hell they've done on the ice that night, or any other night, or what anyone else has done that was right, wrong or indifferent. They use their brains, or what they have of them, to lace up their skates but as soon as they hit the ice, their emotions take over. At the end of the game, they can't remember what the hell they did. Emotions don't have memories. If they did, you'd be perpetually in love with your first girlfriend, which would make future pronouncements of undying love a bit suspect. Just for once I'd like some meathead enforcer with a bloody nose to answer the question of 'what was going through your mind when you smashed the shit out of Jones of the Flames?' with 'what a stupid question.'

And now the most beautiful girl in the world is asking me who the hell I am and all I can do is stare at her.

"Nervous, eh?" she asked. She knew. I nodded. "Well, don't be." She reached across the table and took my hand, stroking my fingers with hers. "Like the wine?"

"Yeah, it's good," I said and took a sip. Her stroking my hand took the panic away. If she bottled that, Prozac would be toast. "What happens now? I mean, do I go get a room or something?"

"No, already done that," she said. "We're in 45A, a penthouse. I used my card. You'll pay back when we leave, okay?"

"Okay."

"So you want to go up?"

I nodded. She put up her hand and the waiter was there, poof, just like that. She nodded, he nodded back, and returned a few moments later with a bill, which he gave to her, not me, and she took a $100 bill and put it on the table and stood up. I followed her out of the bar, marveling at the smoothness of her stride, her whole body, and looking around to see who was seeing what I was seeing. The men, to a one, were watching her, too, and they were smiling. The women were watching the men, and they were not smiling. As we passed through the entrance, she turned to me.

"Know what that was?" she asked. I shook my head.

"The women in there were watching the competition in context and fearing the future. The men were mourning their lost youth. They were watching you and they were jealous as hell, not just because you're with me now, but because they were too busy with their own self-importance twenty years ago to take the time to be with someone like me back then." She pushed the top button on the elevator and the doors swung shut. I realized I still didn't know her name.

"Gillian," she said. *Holy shit! She does read my mind!* "I don't need to know your name but you should know my mine. After all, I can't have you going through life not being able to compare me by name with everyone else, can I?"

"I suppose not," I said, as we stepped onto the 45th floor and she went directly to the room. "This your favorite hotel?"

"No, actually," she said, "I've only been here once before. You can't go back to the same place all the time or the staff figure out what you do for a living. That can be a little difficult."

The room was huge with floor-to-ceiling windows facing south over the city with its twinkling banks and a steady stream of car lights running up and down University Avenue in the distance like slow motion tracer bullets. To the right was a bar and on top was a bucket and a bottle of Moet & Chandon champagne and two wine flutes. A large sofa and a deep farting chair were near the window just beyond it. A desk and chair, like a small teak office, were to far left, also facing the window and the waterfront. In between, nothing but drawn-back curtains stopped you from walking right up and standing on the edge of the city and I walked there and turned around to take in the rest of the room.

To the right, one door, wide open, went into a massive bedroom with an equally massive bed. I walked over. Another door from the bedroom led into a bathroom. A television overhung the Jacuzzi bathtub on the left side. A shower, toilet and double sink arrangement filled a corner. Another door led to *another* bathroom, this one larger. And on the floor were Gillian's clothes. I heard the pop of champagne and went out to see her, wrapped only in a thick white bathrobe, pouring the wine into a flute which she then handed to me. "Now go into the bedroom and get undressed," she said. "Your bathrobe is on the bed. Put it on and come back." She was as beautiful in the bathrobe as she had been downstairs, even though she was hidden from neck to ankles and I couldn't see a bit of skin.

Maybe it was the excitement, maybe it was the hotel, but when I got undressed, I was warm all over and I couldn't feel a whiff of a breeze. You know what it's like when you take your clothes off anywhere else, right? There's always a breeze. It's always colder than when you've got your clothes on. Even in summer, you take your clothes off and feel a breeze and sometimes it's warm in summer but usually cooler and a bit disturbing. But this time, I took my clothes off and it seemed even warmer than it was with my clothes on. And then when I got into the bathrobe, it wasn't hotter as you might expect, but just softer. Even the champagne didn't cool me down, although it was frosty. I drained it and walked out. She was sitting on the sofa looking out over the city. She held her empty glass up and I took it, filled it, mine, too, and handed hers back. She patted the seat beside her and I sat down.

"How do you feel?"

"Great," I said, "and, okay, nervous."

"Don't be. I won't bite. At first. Then I will, I promise. Oh, don't be afraid, it isn't going to hurt." She took my free hand, turned it palm up, gently slid it under her robe until it rested on her breast and then squeezed it a little so my fingers sank into her skin. "How does that feel?"

"Oh, Jeezes you're beautiful. I know, I know I'm probably not supposed to say that, it's business and all but . . ."

"That's okay, Sweetie." She leaned over and kissed me. Softly. Her lips were slightly wet and they gave a little under the pressure. She breathed through her nose. I felt it on my face. I couldn't help it, I closed my eyes and I moaned, just a little, but enough to startle me, and when I did, she exhaled through her nose more strongly, like she was enjoying herself, really enjoying the moment. She leaned away. I saw her eyes. They were opening. She had closed her eyes, too. For some reason, that surprised me. I continued to kneed her breast.

"We are going to go slowly at first," she said, shifting her weight so she faced me more. "I'm going to show you what I am, show you what a woman is. And then we'll make love for the first time. I don't want you to worry about what happens when we first make love. It will be a rush, a hurry, if you know what I mean, but don't worry about it. That's to be expected. But it won't be over, okay? We'll have some more wine. We'll have a shower and then we'll go to bed. More wine, another shower, maybe a Jacuzzi, and then we'll see, but I have a feeling you are not going to sleep very much tonight. Is that okay? Does that sound like a plan?"

"Oh, yeah," I said. At this point, articulation was not an option.

"You must learn to please the woman you're with first. Blow her mind. So few men will put the woman first that if you do, she will let you do anything. She'll sing songs about you for the rest of her life, even if you leave her." She stood and dropped the robe. I was going to get up and put my arms around her but she said, "no, just sit there. No touching."

Gillian slid her hands around her neck, and then to her breasts which she cupped and kneaded until her nipples stood out. "Don't be rough, at least not at first. Be gentle." She snaked her hand down and lightly ran her index finger down and then up, slowly, coming to rest the tip at the top, where she started to circle it around.

"This, Sweetie, is the hood of my clit. The clit is very very sensitive, the hood less so. When you reach down with your hand when you're necking, don't jam a finger in her, rub the hood gently and run your finger up and down like this and press in only when she's wet."

I had the hardest erection I have ever had in my life. I wanted to grab it so bad, but I knew if I did, that would be it. Boom. So I just let it strain against the bathrobe, not daring even to move the tip of my cock against the cloth in case I lost it.

"Boys use their fingers. Men use their tongues. There's not a square inch of a woman's body that doesn't like to be licked and nibbled. Some women want you to say you love them. *All* women want you to say you want to eat them. I want you to lean forward now and kiss and lick my knees, then the inside of my thighs and work your way up, moving as I urge you with my hands, squirms or voice. And then you are going to keep going up and do with your tongue what I did with my finger. I want you to taste me, devour me, lick everywhere. And before you do, I want you to look in my eyes and tell me you want to eat me."

Fifteen minutes into this her hips were twitching violently, she was breathing like she was about to die and I couldn't stop smiling. She grabbed my head, raised her legs and pushed me down further. I licked her asshole. I licked her *asshole!* If I had had the time to think about it, I wouldn't have, but I didn't, and Gillian bucked like it was a brand new experience. She screamed. And then she yanked me up and grabbed me and put it in. She was right about that first time, too. Three strokes in that hot, slippery marvel of flesh and skin and squish and I was done. I shot like a fire hose.

The way she spoke when we started, I thought we'd sort of lie around and talk and maybe smoke a cigarette — her, not me, and I wouldn't have given a shit if she had — and then have a leisurely shower, towel off, go back to bed and slowly get back into the lessons. But as soon as I'd rolled off, she was hauling me out of bed and into the shower and attacking me. I was helpless. The sight of my cum rolling out her mouth as the shower beat down on her head wasn't anything but beautiful. She turned me around, bent me over, reached around and stroked my cock as she licked *my* asshole and I was as hard a steel in seconds.

Nothing was the same twice all night. It was all new. I trusted her completely. I was in a fog. When we finally fell asleep as the sun was coming up, I turned on my side and felt her spoon my back, and I know I was smiling uncontrollably as the world went foggy then black.

The phone screamed. It took all my energy to reach out for it. I didn't want to. I wanted it to just stop by itself but the bastard wouldn't stop and I had to take my arm out from under the blanket, which I resented doing, and grab the receiver and lift it off to shut it up and listen as someone, a woman, said hello on the other end.

"Hello, Sweetie," the voice said. I turned my head quickly. The bed was empty. "Gillian?"

"Hi, Sweetie. The doorbell will ring in ten minutes," she said. "Breakfast will be served."

"What time is it?"

"Ten o'clock. Technically, check out is in an hour."

"Where *are* you?!"

"Going north. Home. In my car."

"Are you coming back?"

"No, Sweetie. I'm on my way home. I'm sorry I had to go so soon but I just did. I actually wanted you to see the most erotic thing you'll see today, too, but time ran out."

"How can we top last night?"

"Getting dressed in the morning. You will know you've met your match when she knows how to get dressed in the morning and leaves you as hard as you were the night before. Slowly. With style and rhythm. A reverse strip. Each time she puts something on, you'll know you won't see it again until, perhaps, that night. Perhaps. She'll slide her panties up and her pussy will disappear. She'll just fluff up the outside a bit and utter a little moan. Her bra will go on slowly. She'll adjust it, cup her breasts, put on a low-cut blouse, bend over. Her toes will extend and slide very slowly into her shoes. You will be panting. You will not be able to think about anything else all day."

"Jeezes, I'm as hard as a rock now and you're not even here!"

"Good. You get the idea."

"Where do you live?" I was panicking now. I was alone. She wasn't with me. I felt lost. I felt like I was in a foreign land somewhere.

"That would be telling, wouldn't it?" she said.

"But I owe you money, don't I?" I said, more to keep her on the line than anything. I felt crass as soon as I said it.

"No, nothing. I took some money from your wallet to pay for the room, champagne and your breakfast. I also took $100 for the bar bill I paid, another $100 for the maid, which is on the side table by the door, and $60 for gas. Sorry, I was almost out."

I made my way over to my pants and riffled through the wallet. I'd come in with $2,500. The room was $1,500 a night, it said on the door. The champagne probably cost another $200. I didn't know how much the breakfast was going to be but I still had more than $700 in bills. "But how much did you take for yourself?" I said.

"Nothing, of course," she said.

"Nothing? Nothing?"

"No, nothing. Did you really think I was a call girl?"

It never occurred to me she wasn't. How was I to know? I'd never hired a hooker before.

"Jeezes, Gillian . . . I hadn't thought about it, I mean in terms other than, you know, you, me, money . . . so I guess I assumed . . . Oh shit. You're not a call girl, but now you're leaving without saying goodbye . . . I mean in person . . . does this mean I can't see you again? I mean, we had a great time last night, didn't we? I should have known a hooker doesn't get into it like that I suppose but now . . . Have I done something wrong?"

"Not at all."

"But what was going on last night then? If you're not a, well, you know, if you're not, then what are you, what do you do?"

I heard a giggle at the other end of the line. "Believe it or not, I sell fishing rods."

"Fishing rods? You're kidding!"

"Nope."

"Then what was all that last night? For the last two nights?"

"Well, I knew you thought I was a hooker when we met. Actually, I was coming out of the Sears building having seen an old friend of mine who works there, and you came up and I knew you thought I was a hooker. Because you thought that, I knew you didn't know a hooker from a fishing rod salesperson, and I have always fantasized about being a hooker, or more precisely a call girl, so I pretended to be one. I figured it would be exciting. And it was. So, you see, we both lived our fantasy last night, and in style, I should say, so we both won. And for two nights because I must say it was fun pretending to be one and I wanted to stretch it out. That was selfish of me, I know."

"Fishing rods? You sell fishing rods?"

She laughed again, hard this time. "Yup."

I took all this in like I was a sieve. The information was going into my ear and spilling all over the carpet. I couldn't keep track of any of it. The whole world had changed three times over the last two days and nights. I panicked again. "Can I see you again?"

"No, no, that would spoil it," she said.

"Please?"

"I'm sorry, Sweetie. It's not going to happen."

I almost wanted to cry. I'm not sure I didn't a little. I can't remember clearly for the next day or so. It was like someone in the family had died suddenly. Here today, gone today. I had so many questions and it was fast becoming clear I would not be able to ask all of them. "But I've got to talk with you again," I said.

"This is it. We can talk until I get home or the batteries fail or I lose my cell connection."

"Last night, in the bar, you said you would not do some things and that I had to promise to stop if you said, No. What were they? I can't imagine what they could be. You never said, Stop."

"Nothing. We did it all. So you see, we both, in our own ways, lost our virginity last night. Thanks. I won't forget you. Ever. Really. You're gorgeous."

The phone went click, and then the dial tone sounded. I'd lost her.

CHAPTER FIFTEEN

When I went down to the front desk, Gillian had paid everything. In fact, there was a $56 credit for some reason, which I told the front desk man to give to the chambermaids.

"Housekeeping, sir."

"Whatever you like," I said.

"Can I get your car?" he asked.

"It's okay. I'm walking."

"I can procure you an umbrella, if you like, sir," he said. I looked outside. In retrospect, it was raining but I'd only had about three hours sleep and I was so confused about Gillian that I was wondering if any of it had actually happened and the last thing on my mind was the weather.

"Thank you, no, I'll be fine," I said, and walked out the front door, past the guy in the gold brocade, and out on the street. One block later, I was freezing and grabbed a taxi. I wished it had been Abdul. I wanted him to know that I was going to be just fine, no matter where I went. I'd seen to it that I would be able to have it all later. But, of course, it wasn't Abdul driving. It was as if he had been there that one day, that he was destined to drive me to Niagara and then disappear forever. I missed him, old Abdul, and I wanted him to know what I'd been up to since we met. I looked for him often. I didn't know his last name and couldn't remember the cab company he worked for. It wasn't one of the big ones.

When I got back home I stripped off my clothes and climbed into bed. I didn't want a shower. I wanted to smell her on me, although, really, I couldn't smell her at all because we had a shower just before going to sleep that morning. All I smelled was the hotel soap, slightly flowery, but not too much. It was still her. Before I left, I'd stuffed my pockets with all the soap and shampoo I could find in the bathroom to remind me of her and that night. It smelled so good.

I wanted to sleep, I guess, or more likely to dream, but I couldn't. I kept fidgeting and smiling uncontrollably. I put on an old movie, a Fred Astaire thing on television, and I tried to follow along but every ten minutes or so I found myself staring at the ceiling and laughing out loud and then I'd go back to watching Fred and Ginger and not knowing what the hell was going on. This went on right through the original Terminator. I wasn't even hungry. It was dark when I finally fell asleep. That's all I remember.

The next morning I felt great. Full of energy. Far from feeling weak at all. And bursting. I kept thinking of Gillian, although it seemed like a long time ago, and even my dick was no longer sore. Reality intruded when the phone rang.

"It's Manny," the voice said. "Your suit is ready. I thought you said you were in a hurry, or something. We did it right away."

"Yes, right, yeah, great," I said. I recognized his voice. It had only been two days, after all. I had the ticket somewhere. I figured for sure this was one of those guys who said 'no tickie, no washy,' but I was probably wrong. How many people take in a clown suit to be cleaned? How could you forget them? "How much?"

"Seventy-four fifty-six."

"Okay, I'll pick it up as soon as I can." I said. I heard Manny sigh.

It's funny the way things happen like that. Here I was busting with the urge to tell someone about Gillian and what had gone on – not the gory details or anything; my father taught me to be a gentleman, after all – but just how *adventurous* it had been. That was the word: Adventurous. And then Manny calls and I had an excuse to go down and see Walter on the pretext that I needed cash to get his suit from the cleaners and while I was there I could tell him everything. God it was good to be alive like this. I hoovered breakfast. I was starving.

The tavern had just opened when I got there at 11:30 and Gerald was behind the bar wiping draft glasses on his white cloth. I had expected to see Walter there, on his stool, waiting for the first cold one of the day, but when I walked in, he wasn't perched on his stool and Gerald seemed a little lost. I sat at the bar and he looked up at me. "What can I get you?" he asked.

"Where's Walter?" He peered at me over the bar like he was myopic and then reared back. "Oh, it's you, kid," he said. "Walter's not here. Well, here's the thing, he's not here any more at all."

"Whad'ya mean?" I asked.

Gerald put the glass down. "Look, his sister's upstairs right now. Go on up. She'll tell you."

I took the stairs two at a time. Walter's front door was open and when I went in, a woman was down on the floor, by Walter's chair, looking for something. I walked in and cleared my throat.

"Oh fuck off," she said without looking around. "Don't give me any grief. I hated the prick but I've got every right to be here!"

"Hello?" I said.

The woman turned her head and squinted at me. "Who are you?" she asked. "I thought you were one of those assholes downstairs."

"Where's Walter?"

"They didn't tell you?"

I shook my head.

"He's passed on," she said.

"Passed on where?"

"He's dead, you idiot. Died two days ago."

"No, no, that can't be. I saw him a couple of days ago. I was right here talking to him."

"Nevertheless," she said, "he's dead. Died right here in his chair, watching the Comedy Channel, as usual."

I didn't believe her. I was standing there. The floor creaked. The room looked the same. I could see the port bottle and the glasses, clean, on the little table. The chest of drawers was there, the kitchen beyond. But I wasn't there. Physically I was, I guess, but it sure didn't seem like I was actually there at all.

"Classic heart attack," she was saying, standing now, looking at me with a cocked head, waiting to catch me from falling, I think. "Here, come and sit down," and she waved to Walter's chair. I shook it off. No way was I going to sit in Walter's mechanical farting chair. We both stood in silence for a while; I don't know how long, but it was awhile.

"Look, what can I do for you?" she asked. I just shook my head, trying, I think, to shake *her* off. "You knew Walter?"

"A little," I said. "I'd just met him, really, but he was a nice guy."

"A clown," she said.

"Yeah."

"A *real* clown," she said.

"Yeah, I know . . . what happened?"

"The guys called me. Walter hadn't come downstairs for breakfast, as usual, so they sent something up and they found him in his chair. They figured he died sometime the night before. The

Coroner said it looked like a heart attack but they're going to do an autopsy. Given his history, the coroner's probably right. He could have died of anything, though. I mean. He was shot."

"Shot? Shot? Someone shot him?"

"No, no," she said, "his body was shot. He was a mess. Had been for years. I told him to clean himself up. He told me to fuck off. After awhile, I just gave up on him. I don't feel bad about it. There's only so much you can do with a clown like that before you give up. He didn't want any help. He wanted to help others, kids mainly, but he didn't give a shit about himself. Destructive personality."

I felt a bit dizzy, weak, and I was afraid I was going to start bleeding all over the place, but I wiped my nose and nothing stained my wrist, and then I felt a little better. "What are you going to do now?" I asked.

She looked around the room. "Well, I guess I'm looking for anything to salvage, anything of value, and I'll give the rest away, but there's not much here. The TV's old, the dishes are chipped, although Goodwill won't mind that, and the pots and pans are useless . . ."

"I've got his suit," I said.

"His suit?"

"Yeah, his clown's suit. He said it was valuable. It's silk and all and I've got it at a cleaners."

"Oh, God, I don't want that!" she said.

"But it's worth a lot," I said.

"To him. To you. Not to me. I don't want to go near it. You keep it. Or sell it. Whatever you want."

"But why?"

"I *hate* clowns," she said. "Scare the shit out of me. Can't stand the thought of them. Can't stand seeing them. Can't stand being around them."

"But Walter, he was your *brother*."

"Yeah and he scared the shit out of me all my life with that getup. Did it on purpose, the prick. Scared the hell out of me. All the time, every chance he got. Later, when we were still talking, way back, he said he learned a lot from me and my reaction to his fucking clowning, that he learned how to tell whether a kid was afraid or not. He said the kids who asked the questions all the time weren't afraid. The kids who didn't ask questions, and were afraid to be asked questions, like me, were afraid. And he said he wasn't sorry he scared the shit out of me. My bother was a selfish prick."

"Wow."

"Right, wow," she said. "You keep the suit. It's yours. Consider it a gift from Walter. And never, ever try to give it back to me, okay?"

"Okay . . ." I didn't know what to do now. I didn't know where this was going. "What if you change your mind," I said, "maybe you should give me your name and number so I can get back to you . . ."

"Don't worry about it. I don't want nothing from you and you don't want nothing from me," she said.

"Is there going to be a funeral or something. I'd like to go to the funeral, if you don't mind."

"No funeral. He didn't want one. He bought a plot and he wanted to be cremated and planted there but only because you have to be planted somewhere. When the coroner's through with him, he's going to go to the funeral home and they'll take care of the rest. No funeral. Nothing."

I felt terrible about this. I mean, not only was Walter gone, just about everything about him was gone, too. I would never see him again and I wouldn't be able to say goodbye. It didn't seem right. She looked up at me. I must have seemed lost. "Go," she said, "there's nothing you can do. Keep the clown suit to remember him, but I wouldn't blame you if you buried it, or sold it and kept the money. A kid like you can always use the money, right?"

I was going to tell her I didn't need it, that I already had money I couldn't spend but it would have just led to questions, or maybe not, given how this woman was acting, but nevertheless, it would not have been productive to let her know I had a ton of gold and it was virtually useless to me.

It all came back again to that camel-though-the-eye-of-the needle Bible lesson thing. If I were caught red-handed with the gold would that mean I couldn't get into the Kingdom of Heaven just because I was rich? Jeezes, I'd never had to think much about money and suddenly it's a huge liability? I liked the cash I made flipping burgers for two summers at The Breeze Bar, because I would plan ahead what I wanted to buy. Figuring out how long I had to work before being able to afford it was fun. And when I'd earned enough, I'd be on top of the world. I liked that money. But the gold didn't do the same thing. It didn't seem legit. I'd given some to Abdul, but he earned it, and I'd spent some on the Casino, which was like throwing it away really, so I didn't really spend it on something I wanted. Or needed. All I did was use it for structural improvements to my bed. The cash? Well, I sort of earned that by being my parent's only son. That's sounds crazy, or Imperial, I know, but it was family money. I was part of the family, so it made it legitimate.

Whatever, I had the feeling that there was a clear difference between money you made yourself and found money and a difference about how you got your money. If you earned it with hard work and you were a good person, unlike the Pharaoh or Caesar, the camel conundrum shouldn't apply. Actually, the thing needed updating. It's a couple of thousand years old anyway, and like Abdul said, stories like that should be passed down through generations and adjusted now and then to suit the times. So I figure that it would be easier for a camel to get through the eye of a needle than for a rich man to *buy* his way into Heaven. That would put things into perspective.

"I guess I'll go then," I said.

"Bye, kid," she said, and then just looked at me, not moving, waiting for me to turn and leave, which I did, slowly, reluctantly.

The day outside had turned shitty. The clouds were coming down over the tops of the buildings, it had turned cold, and the wet air seeped through my clothes and my skin and buried itself in my bones. I felt achy, all of a sudden, a little weak, although when I checked, I wasn't gushing anywhere. Now what was I going to do? I went to see Walter to tell him about Gillian and now I couldn't. I couldn't tell my parents for obvious reasons. And besides, what 18-year-old could tell his parents *anything* of importance without getting the, "you'll learn" speech. I thought of calling up Ralph, my only non-debating nerdy friend at school, and while he would have gotten a kick out of what I'd done, I'd never know whether he really understood the magnitude of the whole thing. This is the guy in the law course about wills who almost threw up when the teacher talked about being *in testate*. When he was reassured that he could avoid the problem by making a will, he said the first thing he would put in it would be, "this is my last will and testament blah blah, and let it be known that no one should cut my cock or balls off for any reason, even organ transplants, despite the thing in my wallet I signed when I got my driver's licence." Ralph was a good guy, just not that quick, and I didn't think he'd quite understand how I really felt about Gillian, or how she wasn't really a hooker. He'd always think she was. It was the only way he was going to get laid for the first time, so he'd think it was the only way I would, too. And besides, now I had to tell someone about Walter and then Ralph really would be lost. I mean, he was eighteen, too, and an eighteen-year-old isn't going to be any good in a situation like that. He'd say he was sorry, mumble something about how he'd do anything to help, but the truth is, he couldn't do *anything* to help. He wouldn't know how. Hell, I didn't know how to help *myself.*

As I stood there outside the tavern, starting to freeze, I realized the only person I could talk to about Walter was Gillian. How twisted is that? I'd gone to talk to Walter about Gillian and now I had to talk to Gillian about Walter. *She* would understand. But I *couldn't* talk to Gillian because I didn't know how to get in touch with her. Not only could I not get in touch with her, she couldn't get in touch with *me*. What if she wanted to? I know, I know, she said she didn't, but still . . . I started to think I'd have to mull that around but I shook off that idea: I didn't have time to mull. Bummer. But even as I was thinking about being bummed out about losing the mulling option, I must have been mulling anyway because it occurred to me from out of nowhere that Gillian might *need* to get in touch with me. What if I'd gotten her pregnant? My brain started spinning. I thought I might have to sit down. It was possible, wasn't it? I didn't use a condom. What was she *thinking!* . . .

All I knew was her first name and that she drove a BMW, she lived north of the hotel and she sold fishing rods. Fishing rods.

Where would you buy a fishing rod? I walked two blocks west to where a big department store was located. The sporting goods area was in the basement.

It's not hard to find fishing rods. They line up like winter twigs jammed into the ground, spaced at a precise distance from one another, waiting for someone, or some fish, to make them bend. They're just long poles with eyelets and cork handles, so when the sales guy came up and asked what I was "fishing for," I thought he wanted a compliment. He was that kind of guy. All sad eyes and his body as long and narrow as the poles themselves. I could swear he wanted me to say I knew exactly why he was here, because he looked the part, more so than the beefy guys in waders and life jackets on TV hauling in bass after bass on those stupid shows, stupid because they go to all the trouble of reeling them in and they let them go. I mean, what's the point? Where the hell are we on the food chain to torture ourselves like that? When you go hunting you 1) never point a gun at anything you don't intend to kill and 2) you eat what you kill. But now we're letting fish go when they've got to be one of the most expensive things in the supermarket. I know. I've got the *Joy of Cooking* and even though fish was never all that popular in our house because my mother didn't know how to cook it, the idea of *Salmon Alsatian* intrigued me until I went and saw how much salmon was. I could have bought a Porterhouse steak for that, which I did, and then kicked myself because I didn't have a barbecue. A porterhouse that big when cooked on the stove requires closed eyes and an imagination to enjoy. I'll bet these guys who catch and release on television go back to camp and have a steak every night and pat themselves on the back. At least they'd have a barbecue.

"May I help you?" the sales guy asked as I fingered this long one.

"Yeah, I'm looking for a fishing pole." As soon as I said it, I knew it was stupid.

"I see, and what type of fishing are you doing these days?" he asked again.

"You know, fish fishing, all kinds of fish."

"Fresh water or will you be traveling south for the Marlin season?"

"Yeah, south. Marlin. Yeah," I said, most convincingly, I thought. "One of your sales people, Gillian I think her name is, told me to come here and ask for her."

"Gillian? Gillian? I don't believe there's anyone here with that name."

"Really?" I said. "Huh."

"But if she's not here, perhaps I can interest you in this one," he said, picking up a humongous pole, which was as thick as my wrist at the bottom and as tall as a mature poplar. "Unless, of course, you're not really here to buy a Marlin pole and you're not really going south for the season and you're . . ."

"That's it!" I said. "Perfect." The bastard was calling me a liar and a fraud so I looked at him like a miser at a TV evangelist. "What's so damn good about that one?"

This seemed to challenge him. In any event, it made me feel better. Like I told you before I think, I hate it when sales guys think they're in charge.

"Well," he said, taking it gently from its stand and eyeing it up and down like he was appraising a model's legs, "it's the control you have with this one. It's got a fighting butt, but it's sensitive. Knowing what goes on at the end of your line is crucial and you always know what's tugging on the end of your line with this baby."

Oh, come on, he's actually talking about a model. Is this guy in my head, or what?

". . . It's made with a IM7 graphite blank with a unique carbon fibre orientation pattern that's extremely resilient."

Okay, now he's out of my thought pattern. What a relief.

". . . And it's only $395.00."

Now, I don't know about you, but buying a skinny poplar tree with eyelets for $395 sounds a bit excessive. How many fish would you have to catch and KEEP, before it paid of, even at wild salmon prices? A whole boat load, I'd say.

". . . unless of course, that's too expensive for you," he said.

Now this dweeb was challenging my inner Hemingway and I was damn sure I wasn't going to let him get away with it. I came in here for a girl and this guy was intimating I couldn't even walk out with a god damned fishing pole? Screw him! "I'll take it," I said.

"Will that be your credit card, sir?"

"Cash!" I screamed. He looked like a scared Ichabod Crane. I knew right away this guy had never had $395 cash in his hands in his life. He spent his entire day running credit cards through electronic scanners. His pay cheque was never a pay cheque, but a direct deposit. This was one of those guys who has never had anything in his pocket but change. I knew, just knew, that when I handed over the cash, he'd have to rely on the till to tell him how much change was due back. I also knew it would cross his mind, as he fingered the crisp bills I had taken from the bank, that he'd consider stealing the cash. No one there would have believed anyone paid cash, no one at the store would know how to recognize it, and he would consider pocketing the bills and scratching his head when someone figured out the store was short. This guy, who was selling me something that would never pay back its investment, was a goddamned thief! I knew it, and he knew it, and I felt better I'd profiled that prick perfectly by the time he had actually given me change (and yes, he did consult the register) and I walked out the door, really carefully, actually, because the thing was huge.

People on the street stared at me. Some smiled. I think I saw someone roll his eyes. But this fishing pole thing was obviously an attraction. Not exactly a chick magnet, or anything, but you *notice* someone walking downtown with a 20-foot pole. A little old lady actually stopped when I was standing there and looked the pole up and down.

"Fishing rod," I said.

"I see that," she said.

"For Marlin," I said. "It's Marlin season down south, you know."

"Not for months," she said, and walked off shaking her head.

I had this feeling I should get out of there fast so I headed to the subway a few steps away. I could take the train and be home in a half an hour and stash the rod.

You take for granted being able to walk down a flight of stairs, turn corners, go through turnstiles and get on subway trains when you aren't carrying a fishing pole. I don't know if you know how tricky it is when you're carrying a 20-foot fishing pole. Let me tell you, it's way harder than you think. Just keeping it upright in areas with low ceilings is a feat, and making sure you don't put someone's eye out by mistake is fraught with anxiety, so when I finally got to the platform with the train standing there ready to go, I had a split second to jump on before the doors closed. In retrospect, it was a poor action choice. I got on, all right. And the doors closed behind me. But most of the rod was left outside the train. Straight outside.

The other thing you might not have noticed is how close the train actually gets to the tunnel walls because, you see, most of the time you're looking around sizing up who's going to mug you, or you're looking at ads on the curved boards above the windows and doors. Trains travel closer than five feet from the tunnel walls, I can tell you, because the tip of the fishing rood was suddenly trying to catch anything on the wall as the train picked up warp speed. At first, the handle sort of jerked in my hand as the train went down the track, jiggling in the rubber things where the doors close. Then it picked up jiggling speed and began to really rattle. It started making quite a bit of noise, too, which is why some people started inhaling loudly but not exhaling. A few seconds later, it was so jerky it was almost coming out of my hand, the tip bent way backward and I saw, about the same time as about a half dozen others on the train, sparks flying off the tunnel wall where the tip was whanging away.

"Oh my god!" someone yelled, "it's going to electrocute someone!"

Well, that was enough for me. I let go of that sucker as fast as I could and now it was whacking the glass partition between the door and the first seats.

"It's going to smash the window," someone else yelled, and everyone in the nearest seats began screaming and lurching to the other side of the train, yelling and trying to keep their eyes in their sockets. Even I stood back in awe and watched the fighting butt whang on the glass like a pneumatic cement cracker. Sparks were flying outside. The graphite blank with unique carbon fibre was holding up admirably, but no one on the train knew about the soft tip and sensitive building materials that one of these state-of-the-art fish-snagging beauties was made of, so none of them knew that thing would hold up under the pressure. Least of all this huge black man who stood up from his seat directly opposite, reached down into his pants and extracted what could only be called a glinting machete, except it was a little smaller, although not by much, and took three steps before raising the weapon of mass destruction over his head and bringing it down like a razor on stubble and slicing the rod cleanly at the door. His follow through would have made Tiger Woods yaw with awe. He then punched the remaining rod out onto the tracks with the blade, slid it back into his pants and sat down. The train erupted. People clapped and shouted. A little old lady, about 600-years-old with bags and sacks and newspapers from four days, stumbled to her feet, walked over to the man and patted his leg. And then, as the train pulled into the next station, and the doors swung open, she turned to me and said in a loud cackly voice, "And you get off this train now!" I picked up the stub of my rod and walked off the train. A cheer went up inside.

Luckily, it was only one stop from my destination. The extra walk was blissfully peaceful.

Chapter Sixteen

Seeing $395 plus tax being scythed like that in a subway train tends to take your mind off things that seemed front and centre a few minutes before so Gillian, or the lack of her, did not prevent me from falling asleep that night. I think an adrenalin overdose pumped me clean of all energy. When I woke up and looked over at the stub of a fishing rod, however, and then pulled out the laundry ticket for Walter's clown suit, perspective once again entered my life. And I felt terrible. It made toast and eggs taste like cardboard and orange juice like chalk. My feet felt heavy. My upper body strength was gone. My eyes were watery. As I sipped the orange juice, I went to the front window and damned if that strange little guy downstairs wasn't going out like a thief again, head down, collar turned up, feet making tiny little steps as if he were chained at the ankles escaping a road gang. What a weird guy.

One of the great things about the Internet is you can ask it to find fishing rod stores and damned if it doesn't. Once you've weeded through the on-line sales, and get actual addresses, then you can get maps and plan your day. I honestly don't know how people lived without computers.

I decided that buying fishing rods in the morning was somehow not right. I don't know why. It just seemed like you should be out fishing in the morning, not buying fishing equipment. Picking up your cleaning seemed more of a morning thing, so I decided to retrieve the clown suit, hit the one fishing rod store between it and my place, dropping off the suit at home and then heading progressively north to hit the other fishing and hunting places, if need be. I wanted to head north rather than downtown because I didn't want to run into those subway guys again if I had any fishing rods with me, especially the machete owner.

It was going to be a long day. It would have been too good to be true to find Gillian right away. Life isn't like that. You have to work hard at it, at least, that's what my father always says, so I had to dress for the inevitable, and that meant jeans and my skateboard shoes. Now, I know what you're thinking; this guy almost always wears Weejuns. I don't *always* wear Weejuns. I wear Weejuns when I need power shoes. You can wear Weejuns just about anywhere and get away with it. It doesn't matter if you wear them on the street or in church, at a wedding or a funeral, in a club or at a bar in the Four Seasons, they work because people look at your shoes and they see money. Not that they cost all that much. But the people who buy them are usually from money, mothers of one carat or better, or people who know people with one-carat mothers and aren't timid about it. But as shoes, they aren't comfortable on the long haul. Skateboard shoes, on the other hand, are the best shoes in the world. You can wear them all day – hell, for three days straight – and they never let your feet down. You can walk for miles in them, except in snow or ice. Traction isn't so good there. But any other type of pavement, or cement or curved drainage pipe will literally stick to the soles of skateboard shoes. By the way, that isn't true about regular running shoes, either. It's well-known they are generally inferior in every way.

Skateboard shoes are also very cool. You can go to this place I know and you aren't even allowed to try them on. You walk in, tell them your size and they go back and see if they have any. If they do, you fork over anywhere up to $1,000 and take them. No returns, either. You can see some real bad asses in there.

Most of mine aren't top-of-the-line. I've got an old pair of *Reynolds Amerika* I use as slippers now, and a pair of *Nike SBs*. If you don't think *they're* cool, you're out to lunch because they're Ferris Bueller shoes. I wear them every day when I'm not wearing Weejuns. My really good ones are still in their boxes in my cupboard at home and I won't wear them now, maybe ever, because they're going to be collectors' items and worth a fortune in the future, I'm sure. So I put on my jeans and my Ferris Bueller *SBs*. I looked good and felt better knowing I was going to be comfortable all day. Shoes are important. Some things parents can teach you, like quantum physics and flossing, but don't try to teach a teenager about shoes. They can run circles around you on that score.

So I stuffed the maps and my laundry ticket into my pants and got to traveling.

Manny was there when I went into the laundry. He didn't look up at me until he read the ticket.

"New clown's here," he yelled over his shoulder. Right away the big aluminum roller coaster started up, whirring clothes around to his back, and within thirty seconds the clown suit appeared wrapped in plastic. Manny ripped the ticket from the plastic and handed it to me: "Seventy-four fifty-six," he said. He stood there staring at me as if I wasn't going to pay. I pulled out a wad and handed him four twenty-dollar bills and he, unlike the fishing rod guy, slipped open a drawer underneath the counter and handed me back $5.44 faster than you could punch the numbers into either a till or a calculator. Manny could add and subtract. He was old school. He didn't need any machine to tell him how much he was getting and how much he should give back and it was, somehow, comforting to know there were people in this world who could still do that. If he had a candy store, Manny would sell candies individually. He was the type who would sell you individual nuts and bolts in his hardware store, a store that stocked all the nails and screws and things in handmade wooden bins along narrow aisles and lit by overhanging bulbs. If he ran a pastry shop, he would make his own bread and cakes and tarts every day and if they ran out by noon, well, he'd close up until the next day. Manny was a wonder. He was a dying breed, a rarity, one of those cars in the Fifties and Sixties with the huge tail fins designed for hope and inspiration rather than performance based upon the pessimism of global warming. Manny handed me the suit, which dangled its plastic on the ground no matter how high I held it, and said, "if you ever see a kid cramming that white cake shit into his pie hole, run for it. It'll save you seventy-four fifty-six."

When I got outside I tied the bottom of the plastic into a knot to make it a bit shorter and then I found that if I put it over my shoulder it wouldn't drag. But that wasn't easy, either. It wasn't heavy but the damn thing kept slipping off my shoulder. I couldn't wait to get rid of it at home but I still wanted to try that sporting goods store that was almost exactly halfway between the laundry and my place, too close to take the subway, not far enough away to justify a taxi. I hoofed it and was there in about ten minutes.

My first impression was they all look alike. Rod racks, that is. I wondered how Manny would display them but couldn't come up with anything, which pretty much summed up my education, I guess. I am a product of the "it's been done" generation. We are presented with something, assume someone has thought it all out before us, and get on using it without thinking about how it could be done better. A few are not like that. They invent. Everyone else uses. A kid gets a computer, he doesn't care how it works, only *if* it works and how to work it. Only if it doesn't produce what he wants does he question it. But he doesn't *do* anything except throw it away or get something else that promises to do what he wants it to do. If it still doesn't produce what he wants, he gets on the Internet and whines about it until someone else joins in and tells him where to get the thing he wants, someone a million, trillion light years away, with no credentials, no history, who is suddenly considered a massively impressive philosopher in the ether devoted to *Individual IT* rather than *Human Understanding*. And as I stood there thinking about this, I thought, *"holy shit, a fishing pole rack has a lot of power in it if you only thought about it!"* Then I thought, *"what a moron I am."* I was getting off track a lot these days.

I was purposefully fingering a starter fishing pole, priced at $9.95, and looking around the store for Gillian, when the guy approached me. "My nephew," I said. "He's six-years-old. His birthday is tomorrow and he told me once he wanted to learn how to fish. Something about Sunday school."

"Well, this will do, of course, but you might want to consider something a little more substantial, something more advanced, to really get him to appreciate the sport."

"Nah," I said, "this woman, Gillian is her name, told me to start small like this. She works here, I think, selling fishing stuff?"

"No, no one here by that name," he said. He saw my disappointment I think because he piped right in, "But, of course, she may know what nephews like yours need better than me. This might just be perfect. But naturally you'll want some line and hooks, lures, bobbers and a tackle box to put it all in?"

"Of course, yes, naturally," I said.

That's the thing about lying. You go in to spend less than ten dollars and come out fifty-six bucks lighter. When I got home, I hung the suit on the lamp in the living room; I wanted to see it, not stuff it into a closet and forget it. I wanted to remember Walter, I guess. And I simply put the new fishing pole and tackle box in the corner of the room by the front door with the half pole from my adventure the day before. I took out my maps and planned the rest of the day.

When I went into the second store, I was pumped. I was certain this was the type of place Gillian would work at because it was clean and classy. But I was also prepared for the sales guy if she wasn't there and somehow, the guy didn't really convince me she wasn't. He seemed like a possessive sort, the kind of guy who thought she was really his and wanted to protect his territory from some other guy walking in there. So I let him sell me another starter pole for my nonexistent nephew but I outsmarted this prick because I told him I was merely *replacing* a pole my nephew broke reeling in a huge smallmouth bass. I have no idea how I came up with a small-mouthed bass. But bass and smallmouth it was, as fast as you could say Marlin. And then I stood around talking about fishing rod sales people, trying to draw him out. If he were, in fact, protecting his territory I thought I could get a rise out of him by saying, "yeah, no broad is ever going to know about fishing. They can't even stand putting a worm on the line." But the bastard just agreed. And I felt like a shit for dissing Gillian, even if I wasn't really dissing her because she wasn't there, but I felt like she *could* have been there, and she *could* have because she sold fishing rods somewhere else, and here I was tearing her down when all I wanted to do was hold her and kiss her and, yup, *thank* her for having my baby. God yes!

At the next place I showed the guy the pole I bought at the first place and said the other place had run out and I needed one just like it for Johnny's friend who was coming to the cottage. It was a good story, but it came with line, hooks, and bobbers because, after all, you couldn't very well share those. *Shit!* The third place was the "sold out at the other place story" but this time it was for the new cub scouts in the troop and they had enough lines and hooks and bobbers and sinkers, even a canoe or two, but needed just one more pole. I had hit upon the right story. Three more stores, three more $10 poles. No Gillian. It was only when I got home and stacked the corner with the now seven and a half fishing poles that I might have just gone to the stores and walked around the parking lots to find a convertible BMW with red leather seats. *What a moron! What a goddamned moron! How stupid can you be?*

It was a trigger of some kind, I think. I got into a real funk. I started to think about Gillian, of course, but also about Walter, then Abdul and the Casino and the girls I met whose friends trashed my place, and the hangover. And what did I have? Nothing. Zero. Nada. I didn't know where Abdul was. Walter was dead. I hadn't found Gillian. The Laundromat girls? Well, I could go back there but, really, what was the point? I had Gillian. *Shit!* I had the *memory* of Gillian, nothing more now. *Shit!* And then I started to think about the worst thing I probably could have thought about. Time.

I might not have *time* to find Gillian. I probably wouldn't have *time* to find out where Walter was buried or go to see his grave. I'd never have *time* to find Abdul, and even worse, I wouldn't have *time* to find out whether Abdul really knew something or not about, you know, what happens when it's over, whether getting water from the villagers down the mountain is worth it if you don't get out of the battle alive. It wasn't as if I could go to some theological retreat to see whether the Anglicans had this Paradise thing straight. And then I thought that if I didn't have time to study something like that, I didn't have time to do just about *anything*. It was all so depressing.

But all day, intermittently, I also thought about having a roast chicken with potatoes for dinner but in the end I never got a chicken. Nothing in the fridge. I didn't have the energy to go out for something and besides, the supermarkets were closed by the time I started acting on it. I didn't want to order in pizza and ordering in chicken seemed like surrender. I sat on my bed and looked around at the walls and some dirty clothes on the floor and I could feel my ass melt into the mattress and cement there. The place seemed cold. Not in the decor sense, but the physical sense as if the furnace quit. I don't know, but the air seemed thicker. It was harder to breathe somehow. A shiver went up my spine, enough to get me off the bed. I looked up at the ceiling and just started to wander around the place thinking about Gillian and Walter and sometimes Abdul. I don't know how long I walked around, but it was dark when I looked out the front window and saw the Dungeon Dweller sneaking down the side alley wearing a thin white coat. In weather like this? And he was pushing this cart that, under the street lights, had writing on the side you could see that said "HT – Caution: Hot." It looked like one of those ovens where subway shops bake their "fresh" bread, which everyone knows is frozen dough thrown into one of these computerized heaters with glass fronts to produce long skinny foam rubber loaves in various colors.

What a weird guy. He didn't make me feel better. Actually, for some reason, the sight of this guy made me feel even worse, as if just seeing him would do something to me, something I didn't want to happen.

At that moment, the place got even colder. My feet were frozen, and so were my hands and the tip of my nose. I went back to the bed and drew the blanket around my shoulders and I started to shiver violently, you know, like when you're a kid and you've been swimming in the water for too long and your teeth begin to chatter and they chatter so much that you let them; you hold them just so far apart so that when you shiver, they clack like those crazy trick teeth?

And as I was doing this, I thought, *Jeezes that was a long time ago, that was when I was a really little kid.* And just like that, I started to cry. Like before. No warning. Tears rolling out of my eyes. Mouth curling like the shivers at the corners. Nose running. I grabbed a tissue and blew my nose and I felt it, somewhere beneath both eyes, a vein popping, and the blood just started gushing out. I didn't have time to get the measuring cup. I put the whole box of tissues over my nose and mouth and let it drain into the box. At one point, as I got to my feet to go into the bathroom where I couldn't stain the carpet, I reached into the box to ruffle the tissues like it was an air filter in a car engine so they would absorb more and not just let the blood roll off the top or through the cardboard bottom. As I sat down on the toilet I felt the trickle down the side of my face and I knew my ears had blown out, too. And all I could do was sit there and bleed. This time there as no humor in it all.

I haven't a clue how long I was there. By the time everything calmed down, and I had stuffed my ears with toilet tissue, the Kleenex box over my nose weighed about a pound. When I got up, I realized I hadn't blown out my asshole this time. Don't know why. I was sure that was going to happen, too, and I couldn't get my pants down. I was just resigned to ruin my underwear and pants and had even figured out how to bag them and throw them away. It seemed important at the time. But when I did get up, I was dizzy. I stumbled a bit as I left the bathroom. One of the only things in the fridge was orange juice so I poured a glass and drank it right down. It helped. I crawled into bed and pulled the covers up to my chin.

And then, just as I was rubbing my head deep into the pillow, that bastard downstairs killed the kid. Or the cat. But he killed something, and it took some time, and then there was that awful silence. In less than five minutes a maniac had terminated my entire world. He took complete control, put me in a position I *had* to accept and act upon, something I had spent all my time avoiding. I had no choice.

Humans, to the exclusion of all other forms of life, have to account for their dead. They have to recognize them, catalogue them, and file them. You can't leave them at the side of the road, you must know what killed them, you must document them so their paper lives can forever be unnecessarily retrieved. It is disgustingly ironic that in civilized societies it is unthinkable to ignore the dead but the dying are routinely neglected, shunned or hidden away if they are poor, sociality unclean or economically inconvenient. The bastard downstairs brought all this home. I couldn't ignore it. The life I had so carefully and happily invented would be over because I had to expose this daemon or cope for the rest of my miserable life with a festering boil of shame. And shame often attaches itself like Velcro to everyone who cares about you. I thought about my parents. I dared to think about Gillian.

Time was crushing me. I needed time to find Gillian. It was being stolen. The last scream, the last whimper I heard, drove me to accept the idea that Dr. Pho was right, after all, that my body had been telling me all along with the Gushes. That meant that there would be very little time, if any, to do anything afterward.

You couldn't stop time, could you? No, you couldn't. But if the Bishop and Abdul were right, maybe God could. If you believed, of course. Maybe I did, maybe I didn't. If I didn't, there was no use thinking about all this shit. But maybe I could hedge my bets and believe for a few moments that He did exist and ask him to stop or slow time. All I wanted was time to find Gillian, so much so that I was willing to do anything. So I got down on my knees. The sun was streaming through the front windows so brightly it hurt, so I closed my eyes tightly:

"If you just give me enough time to find her, then I'm okay with this dying thing, God. Really. Nobody needs to know you're doing this immense favor for just one person, do they? If you stop time, everyone's stopped, and then when you unstop time, they'll just go on like nothing happened because they won't know anything happened because it'd be like they were asleep. It wouldn't be public like turning water into wine, or burning a bush in the middle of nowhere. Okay, so you just stop time and I'll go find Gillian and I won't, like, dog it or anything. I'll be fast. Committed. Focused. I just have to see her again. Seriously just give me that time. That's *all* I want. That's *not* too much to ask, is it? You're God, for God's sake!"

It was one of those lost moments, like the ones during *The Bleeds* when I never knew how long I'd been sitting on the can. I can't remember if I was listening for something, whether I heard it, whether I saw anything or was meant to. Eventually, though, my knees went to sleep, I opened my eyes and I saw a spider crawling into a corner of the ceiling above the bathroom door and, only God knows why I suppose, but I got so bloody scared I fell over onto my side and shook uncontrollably. I looked to the front window. It was dark outside. I slammed my head on the floor. Fucking time *had* stopped. It had *fucking stopped!*

"That's not funny, not fucking funny at all!" I screamed and slammed my fist on the floor. But that hurt. I think I heard a bone break and the pain streaked up my arm and damn near paralyzed me. "You asshole!" This time the tears came but they came from rage not depression. I was so fucking angry:

"All right, all right, I'll go down t the basement, and if that bastard is killing, or has killed some kid, even a god damned cat, I'll kill the bastard myself, and I'll do it screaming your name and it'll be on your head. But if there's nothing down there, I'm going to say I'm very sorry and get t hell out of there and then write a book about what a prick your are. Got it? *Got* it!"

I put on my skateboard shoes. For traction.

CHAPTER SEVENTEEN

As mad as I was, I was scared to go there. You'd think that's crazy because what was the worst thing that could happen? I could die? But I was going to die anyway. You'd think that would be the ultimate *don't give a shit* Confidence Moment, right? But no, I was scared.

I went out my front door, down the alley and found myself in front of an aluminum door opening to a sea-blue concrete floor, which led to a really narrow set of steps with virtually no head room for anyone more than five feet tall. Even though I stepped inside voluntarily, it still felt like some trickster was gently shoving me into the throat of a lizard. I won't lie to you, it was seriously creepy. I'd never seen the face of the guy down there, or talked to him, but I still had a pretty good idea he was somebody who spent his time cutting people up and liking it. He always looked like he was slinking around the edges of a kiddie pool. I paused to think this all over again.

I had to see for myself, of course. If I called the cops and was wrong, not only would I have blown my anonymity but some sick social worker straight out of his theoretical college would suggest, rather forcibly I bet, that I am mentally screwed up and should be chained to a sleigh bed in my parents' home or locked up with the loonies. If, as I think I said before, that bastard *was* killing some kid, he would get his but that would still end my plans to cram everything I could into my life. And that wasn't goddamned fair! My only hope was if I went down there and he wasn't doing anything bad, then I could just say 'sorry to disturb you' and go on with life.

When I look back on it, I should have been at least slightly grateful for being able to determine how things would end. I don't think many people get that chance, except maybe suicides. Old Walter had plans, but he keeled over one night without warning. And what about those villagers? They get lucky enough to have some water and wham! Abdul and his friends come down and beat the shit out of them. And then there's Ivan, or I should say, was.

I crept in and down the narrow steps, bumping my head only once and came to a basement door at the bottom. It was ajar and through the open crack, a steady rush of hot air hummed. At first it seemed slightly refreshing, given my cold state, but as I pushed it open a little to get in, the air started to get wet, almost like a fine foggy summer mist. And once I'd stepped in, I was faced with a plastic curtain, one of those filmy white things that hang down from the low ceiling like lasagna noodles big enough for giants. I pushed through those until I found myself in what you might call a foyer, but only because it was where you'd find a foyer. This one was far from being inviting. It was short and narrow, leading to a door frame and then a short corridor with only one door at the very end. The thing of it was, though, something transparent and viscous was flowing slowly down all the walls, like liquid soap maybe. That stuff came from nowhere and it pooled into floor drains that looked like air vents and they made sucking sounds when they got too full, vacuuming the goop out to clear the grates for more liquid sliding down the walls. A gurgling sound came from somewhere, but I wasn't from the walls. It seemed to come from the room at the end. And then I notice a squishing sound like someone slicing open a watermelon, and someone scraping, maybe with a trowel.

As I said: seriously creepy. I walked as quietly as I could into the corridor. I think I must have been shaking like a condemned man being led to the gallows. The room in the distance looked as if it were glowing red. A nightclub, maybe. Then I heard a pulsing sound: Thump wheeze, thump wheeze, thump wheeze. And the strangest sound of all, music. Classical music. I don't know classics except when I hear them, but this was a symphony with all the players, all the base, all the string, horns and a piano. It had to be a disc. I imagined I might find a DJ in the room, maybe a bar. A bar would be nice. Since the infamous night with the Laundromat girls, I hadn't wanted a cocktail of any kind but now it seemed like a good idea. I even thought I smelled alcohol. It didn't have any particular smell but I knew vodka didn't have much of a smell, unlike Gin, which had a juniper berry smell, or scotch with that rotting earthy thing going for it. But if this were a vodka smell, it had seeped into the walls themselves, because it was strong.

I'm glad I had my skateboard shoes on because as I crept down the hallway, the air got moister and the floor got wetter. By the end, the floor was coated with an inch of greasy slime, like Vaseline, and I almost slipped and fell. It was then that something thwapped against my shirt, like a wet rag, and when I looked down, my shirt was stained, like I'd been coated with a bucket of thick rust. It was cold, too, and as fast as it was wet, it got dry and stiff. Weirder still, and way more scary, my left arm got really hot and then went numb. I couldn't lift it up. It was stuck to my side and weighed a ton. My eyes started to get heavy, I was standing there, getting really, really scared but instead of making my heart race and my adrenalin pump, I felt like I was falling asleep.

I had to move or fall. My feet started to move but I wasn't moving them. They were moving themselves toward the room at the far end with the red light and I couldn't do anything about it, and the closer I go to the room, the stronger the smell. It was actually a stench now and way hotter by the time I got to the entrance of the room and looked in.

I wished I *had* fallen asleep. That crazy bastard had his back to me and a big square piece of metal in his hand and he was plastering the far wall with this red bloody film and the wall was lumpy and then I saw it. A face trying to scream through the red goop in his mouth. Trapped on the wall. The eyes were wild but I knew, even as he looked out at me, that he was dying fast. If things couldn't get more weird, the boy looked a bit like me but where my left eye drooped a bit, his right eye looked saggy. I thought I was going to throw up. It wouldn't have mattered a bit if I had, either, because the floor was swimming in snakes and eels and ropes and that same goo the crazy bastard was troweling over this kid's face. He couldn't hear me over the wheezing noise and music through the speakers in the ceiling.

When I looked to my left, there was an old stove and on it was a cast iron frying pan. I grabbed it with my right hand, and when my feet moved me close enough, I swung the pan as hard as I could at his head. It bounced off his skull and he whirled around, grabbing the side where I connected. His mouth was open but before he could speak, I swung again and down he went in a heap, almost swallowed by the goo and the snakes and the ropes and the eels crawling all over the floor. Then I grabbed the phone on the wall beside the stove and dialed 911.

CHAPTER EIGHTEEN

I don't think hedging bets is pathetic. I think it's more like buying life insurance; there's a good chance it's a complete waste of money but if you can *afford* to buy it, the odds are maybe a little better than the lottery. Not much, but better. And like a lottery, you're really investing in hope, aren't you? I mean, you don't expect to kick off suddenly, and you probably figure you're invincible when you sign up, but then again, look at me. I've already told you what my parents think about lotteries. I'm actually afraid to ask at this point whether they're still firm on their anti-hope stance, especially after I went out and tried to get a new life and it didn't work out perfectly.

I've left out a few things that maybe you should know about. Maybe not. But it's not as if I'm going to be able to add some things or correct others later on. I have accepted the fact that Dr. Pho was right, I'm on my way down as fast as a mudslide blah, blah, blah. No use in denying the obvious: I'd be an idiot if I did. But, like I said earlier, it's this time thing. I'm just not going to have enough time to figure a lot of stuff out so I'm going to hedge my bets on a lot of it, like what happens after I croak.

This is the hedging part. In case Abdul is right and you go to Paradise in one piece, I made a list of some things I'd like up there, or wherever it is, other than the stuff I've already mentioned. I'm thinking maybe you have to go on record about everything before you die. I'm not going to bore you with it. It's long. And with things like music from Dylan, Arlo Guthrie, Cream, and Crosby Stills Nash & Young, hopelessly my parents' music, I'd look even more like the nerd I have come to embrace in myself. My food likes are, in contrast, highly sophisticated, if I might say so myself, but because I'm not going to show you my list here, you'll never know how deluded I am in this regard. The only problem I foresee if Abdul's got it right is that I might not get bacon in Paradise. If the Anglicans are in charge and it's Heaven, I'm set for those BLTs at lunch.

I was right about the cops. They sent me home. They knew about the gold but since I didn't actually steal it, and only "lost" a few in transit, and I was willing to tell them everything, especially what I didn't see, namely how Ivan and the robbers ended up dead, no charges were laid. By the way, they knew all about old Walter and seemed genuinely sad that he, too, had died. One said the neighborhood wouldn't be the same without Walter and Ivan. Hell, the entire city won't be the same without them. I think they should put up a "Tomb of the Unsung Characters." Everybody makes such a fuss about "diversity" as if race, religion or country of origin is a big deal in Toronto. Twenty years ago, maybe, but now? Toronto should grow up. It's what weird things go on *inside* people's minds that's diverse, not what the hell they look like. But in defining the city by its population, we've been unthinkingly trained to look through the lens of a TV camera to see who were are. And unless someone talks in suitable sound bites, we don't hear them. The clue here is what we don't hear. People say fuck, shit and asshole all the time. You never hear that on televison. They bleep it out. They're bleeping out reality. They're giving you a picture of some ideal world that's been cooked up in a boardroom. You sit in your farting chair, watch and say, "yup, that's our world" but it's not, goddamn it. Walter would look great on TV, sound great, too. You'd never know he was drunk or had a plate in the back of his head, or that he lived to make kids laugh. The census would have labeled Ivan as a hardworking shopkeeper in a marginal service on Church Street. His essence was his artistry and a healthy disregard for asinine laws. He practiced social disobedience with aplomb. His picture would tell you none of this. His voice would only be allowed as a bite for as long as it took to label him in terms of religion or ancestry. And that bastard downstairs? He'd look like a surgeon on TV!

You know I've been wrestling with finding a way of getting the camel through the eye of a needle, right? Well, now I've boiled it down. I figure that way back, when Matthew wrote it down, it was a battle between good and evil, black and white. The majority was poor and downtrodden, the rich were the downtrodders. But in those days, they didn't have computers or even radio and you can't expect a lesson to spread to everyone through word-of-mouth unless it's catchy and simple. The catchy part is the camel and the needle. The simple part is if you're rich, you're out of luck. You can't say, ". . . easier . . . than for a rich man, with notable exceptions like you're not a bad guy, to enter into the Kingdom of God." It wouldn't fly. Everyone would get it wrong. The problem with it is the lesson was too damn good. We still remember it. Even me. It's become a huge debate for guys like Injun Joe and Chinky Chen: Good versus bad, weak versus strong, serfs versus dictatorships, liberals versus conservatives, communism versus democracy. All that is bogus. It's way off topic. The truth is, it's still all about money. When you're young, no matter where you live, you probably haven't got much money so you think all rich guys are suspicious. You side with the camel. When you're older, you've probably got a realistic handle on money and know trying to buy your way into Heaven is just a concept. But Chinky Chen and Injun Joe could still debate about the fringe elements of society: Be it resolved that those who are obsessed with money for money's sake and have been bastards getting it, or those who've won the lottery, will always try to get the camel through the eye of the needle. Freeze dry it, maybe.

I left something out at the beginning, or nearly the beginning of this diary that, I'm not exactly proud about. Remember when my mother and I were in the doctor's office and he told us I had something seriously wrong with me and my mother, in an instant, went from this completely together mother to a mess? It was awful to see. I felt like shit and I hadn't said a lousy word. Three carats to a puddle in two seconds flat. She eventually pulled herself together as I studied the parking lot and asked, "are you sure, doctor?" and he said he was sure, well, pretty sure, but the only way to really know would be to open me up, look, remove whatever bad they found and then go from there. I sort of remember the conversation going around and around about the positives and negatives of the whole procedure and that sometimes the negatives were worse that just leaving it alone and my mother was wringing her hands and looking at me like she had never looked at me before and I thought we'd be there for years so I said, "Okay, let's find out for sure." Two days later they put me under, carved, looked, and closed me back up right away. The whole thing took maybe an hour. Now my mother knew and, really, that's what the whole exercise was for. I knew, too, of course, but what I couldn't get my head around – and, in fact, didn't believe – was that just opening me up could speed up the whole dying process. I'm not sorry I made that decision. But I am sorry now I didn't mention that at the beginning of my scribbling but I wanted you to read it. If you knew, really knew, what was going to happen and why I was doing everything so fast, I don't know if you could have stayed with me. I mean, it could be considered morbid and if you passed this over and said, "you've *got* to read this, it's *so MORBID!*" how many would actually take it off your hands? It's probably dishonest diary-wise, but, hah ha, it's too late now, isn't it?

So here I am now, back in my parents' house. First thing I wanted was my mother's egg salad sandwich. I had about fifty of those, and I made her make so many because somehow she found the recipe and after the second one, I knew I could count on them. Damn, they were good! And I made her roast a chicken and make some spaghetti, as well. They were great, too. It was a Jewish chicken, she told me. She didn't need to; I knew from the first bite.

They moved the sleigh bed back in and brought me my laptop to write this. At first I could sit up with pillows behind my back and type away but I started to get weak again. So they got me this foam thing that looks like the top of an arm chair, as if you cut the top off the farting chair, and put it behind my back. That way I could rest my elbows on the padded arms and keep myself upright. It was hilarious, though, because I'd fall asleep and slide down but the thing would keep my arms up above my head so I looked like I was doing that Club Med "hands up, baby, hands up" song and dance, except I was asleep and probably snoring and drooling. I asked my parents to take a picture of it. When I asked the first time, my mother put her hand up to her mouth as if she were going to throw up. No sense of humor about all this, I guess. My father eventually took a digital of it and made an inkjet print but said I had to hide it and he had to delete the original from the camera or my mother would kill him. I agreed. No use in two thirds of the family disappearing at roughly the same time.

I also asked that when they put me down, so to speak, that they dress me in the clown suit. The thing is, I *am* only 18, which is sort of between being an adult and a kid, and I sort of feel in between, too. On the one hand, I'm really happy I got laid and I got to drink everything from good wine and booze to port, so if Abdul is right, I can be an adult in Paradise, or whatever it is, if indeed there is one. But I would also like to be a kid when I want to. And if I had the clown suit, I could play with the kids as an adult without looking like a perv doing it. If you're an adult, you can't go round playing with little kids. You'll get arrested, even in Heaven, I'll bet. But if you're dressed like a clown, you *can*. So I asked my parents to dress me in the clown suit but to be honest, I don't think they will. I hope that at least they pack it up with me, though, because then I can change into it. And maybe that's a better plan, but still, I think it'd be hilarious if they put it on me and had an open casket. And then there's the Walter bit. If Abdul is right, Walter might be there and want the suit back. It's clean, after all. I paid for the cleaning so maybe I can borrow it some time.

I'm still wrestling with the whole Fate thing, though. Did what happen to me happen because I *made* it happen, or did all those things *make* me do them and go where I went, or did Fate or God enter into this picture? Or did my illness make me do whatever I did? But who made me sick in the first place? Who would make an 18-year-old sick like that? That's getting damned close to a mental Black

Hole, isn't it? The bottom line is, though, I remain seriously confused. I'm pretty certain Jackson Pollack was shot dead because I had the gold to prove it. Pretty sure. And how should I have reacted to his death? Was he a Chinky Chen kind of guy or an Injun Joe guy? He did very bad things. Ivan's relatives, if he had any, would remember Jackson Pollock as a monster. But almost all his neighbors told the news guys they had no idea they were living beside a stone cold robbing killer. To them he was a quiet guy who kept to himself and seemed friendly. Once he picked a kid up who had crashed his tricycle and took him home. See what I mean about TV news reality? If Injun Joe is right, then the Fates or God made him bad. Now that's not very comforting either, is it?

I'd like to think Walter was more of a Chinky Chen kind of guy whom we can all remember as a clown who loved kids and didn't really want anything from anybody, more of a giving sort. But those cleaners didn't like him; he must have done something bad to them so maybe . . .

The biggest "what if," however, was Gillian. Was she real? She appeared out of nowhere and then disappeared. She was perfect, and how many people can you describe as perfect? But it really got confusing when I thought of her in terms of being an "angel" because she was to me. Now I was in deep shit mentally and back in Injun Joe's camp because what Fate or God would work with people as different as Jackson Pollack and Gillian? I mean, they both were thrown at me somehow. I didn't wake up and say, 'I'm going to go downtown to Church and meet a real hard-ass bastard and an angel. You could try to do that for the rest of your life and you'd *never* run into the characters on demand like that. So Injun Joe must be right,

right? But if you had a choice between playing with Gillian or Jackson, what Fate in his right mind would choose Jackson? Then an idea came into my head and it changed everything.

Have you ever had one of those ideas where suddenly you just sit up straighter and smile? That's the kind of thought I had. Everyone always speaks of one God, or Fate as a single thing, right? But what if there are all sorts of Gods and Fates? One got off on Gillians, another on Jacksons. Maybe they play a sort-of cosmic game and pick a subject like me, and throw stuff at him, betting against each other what the subject, namely me, will do? And how do they know who wins? Chinky Chen! How I react and what that does to people I meet from then on is how I'm judged, right? It was brilliant! Sometimes I amaze myself.

It was a comforting theory, too, until I started thinking about how I reacted to everything. After the Jackson Pollack incident I'd become a thief, not exactly like him but in theory, I guess. But at least I'd made Abdul happy. They could interview him, if they could find him, and he'd be cool. But I hope no one smelled me as I ran home. I'd shit my pants, after all. And I sure as hell hope they don't interview the little old lady on the subway after the Marlin fishing pole incident . . . I was getting more than a little confused thinking about all this when it got just too damn tiring.

I have to admit, in such a short period of time, I met a lot of weird people, saw a lot of new things, and did a lot of things I never would have. Death is a great motivator.

I had a lot of time to think, as you may have noticed. It wasn't all fun and games, although, really, a lot of it was. A couple of things became pretty obvious about this Life and Death business. The big difference is Life begins once and only once, as a wonderful paralyzing spasm in the Four Seasons Hotel, if you're really lucky. On the other hand, Death comes in a thousand ways. As you can see, the deck is stacked. Death is almost always a big surprise for some irrational reason. I mean, you know it's coming, you just don't know the exact time and what the doctor will write as the cause of death. What we do between the two as the cards are flipped over is choose between feeding the body, the mind and/or the soul and I think if you look around, you can see where the food is going with people. Jackson Pollock starved his soul to feed his body; his mind was not a functioning organ. Walter starved his body to strengthen his mind and soul, I'd like to think. Gillian fed everything in perfect moderation; body, mind and soul, she had it all.

Soon after, when I was more or less permanently in bed, the parade of moaners started coming by, friends from school, old babysitters except for Judy, the only one I was interesting in seeing, relatives I saw only once a year at Christmas who didn't know me from shit, all standing by the side of my bed saying exactly what I knew they would say, crap, and the dreaded, "if there's anything I can do," phrase that meant they had no clue what was going on. Some of the girl cousins were hot, and I would have done them had I known what I know now. But then there's that stupid reality thing again; would I have done them or, more to the point, would they have let me? Or even more importantly since my revelation, would some Fate or God give them to me?

One of them in the parade was the Anglican priest my mother sent for, even though I knew he was there for her, not me. The Bishop couldn't make it so it was this young one. I have to say I was a bit insulted that she thought my soul needed saving but if anyone should know, I know that life is too short to get pissed off about things like that. I asked the priest what he thought about my multiple Fates and Gods theory, after going through everything that happened to make me lean toward it. He got a bit flustered. He said the Greeks and Romans thought the same way but God sent Jesus down to whip them into shape. I said I found it hard to dismiss them because the Greeks and Romans weren't primitives, after all. Why do we embrace the philosophy and democracy of Greece and revere the power and invasion strategies of the Roman Legions but dismiss their ideas of multiple Gods? Why could those civilizations build houses that have lasted for thousands of years while home builders today only guarantee their homes for seven years tops? He said the subject was a big one and it would take time to discuss. When I pointed out I didn't have much of that, he apologized. He never did answer me. I wonder what he'll think when he sees me in a clown suit at the funeral?

Anyway, I'd like to go on some more but that's about all I can do. The Clydesdales are getting restless. Every day they start stomping their huge hooves earlier and earlier in the day and turning around and looking at me as if I should do something, or tell them something, but I don't really know what to say. Not really. I have an idea but you know, I think they'll figure it out. We haven't been together for all that long, but we've seen a lot together and from the amount of time I have spent in this bed, I think they'll know when they can charge off. Actually, I'm counting on it. I don't want the morphine to do it. I want to grab the reins, give them a shake, and say

"Giddy-up." That's what I'll do. Gods, Fates, Prophets, or whatever, willing.

THE END